Praise for Kevin David Anderson's

Night Sounds

"Kevin David Anderson's short stories are nightmare-provoking, with a sly mixture of cleverness and humor that makes you snicker when you probably shouldn't be."
—Theresa Halvorsen, author of *River City Widows* and *Warehouse Dreams*

"If darkness calls your name, these stories are written just for you! Like a siren's song, this collection draws you in and then delivers heart-stopping moments of terror."
—Evan Baughfman, author of *The Emaciated Man* and *Vanishing of the 7th Grade*

"What an incredible collection. Anderson does an amazing job creating characters you care about and fantastical murderous monsters, thrusting them into horrific situations and finding a nice blend of humor and brutality."
—Markus Tullius, author of *Untold Mayhem* and *Twisted Reunion*

"Palpitating fun. Kevin David Anderson's *Night Sounds* delivers!"
—R W Goldsmith, author of *The Serpents of Eden* (2023)

Also by Kevin David Anderson

Midnight Men: The Supernatural Adventures of Earl & Dale

NIGHT SOUNDS

From Podcast to Print

Kevin David Anderson

A
GRINNING SKULL PRESS
Publication
PO Box 67, Bridgewater, MA 02324

DEDICATION

To William Anderson

A creative person could not ask for a more encouraging and supportive father.

CONTENTS

ACKNOWLEDGMENTS

I'd like to thank Norm Sherman for selecting many of my stories and being the first to give me a wider audience on his outstanding, strange, and bizarre podcast, The Drabblecast. I'd also like to thank the fine folks at Pseudopod for producing my stories for their literary horror fans. And a big thank you to Rish Outfield and Big Anklevich for featuring some of my horror tales with their customary comic irreverence on their, now gone but not forgotten, podcast The Dunesteef (Don't ask what it means, nobody knows.). A huge thank you to Mr. Jason Hill, who not only breathed new life into many of my stories on The Horror Hill podcast but is responsible for popularizing and giving voice to my two favorite characters, Earl and Dale. Thank you to Otis Jiry, who has voiced a half dozen of my tales for his creepy podcast, Otis Jiry's Scary Stories Told in the Dark. I'd like to thank the folks at The Night's End podcast for producing my stories down under, giving my stories an amazing and distinguished Aussie sound. I'd like to thank Fred Greenhalgh and his FinalRune Productions for doing a live, full-cast, radio drama-styled production of my story, *Third Shift*, on Halloween night. I'll never forget it. Thank you to the podcasts that are no longer with us that produced many of my tales, like the Chicago-based Sniplits and Kevin Colligan's Well Told Tales. More recently thank you to the producers of the creepypasta-styled show, The NoSleep Podcast for producing some of my first-person narratives and sending my work out to the largest audio audience to date. A big thank you to the fine folks a Grinning Skull Press for helping me put together and publishing this collection of former audio stories.

And finally, to all the long-gone radio stars and producers of what we now call old-time radio. This author spent many preteen nights, laying out under the stars listening to rebroadcasts of *Lights Out, Dimension X, Escape, Suspense, Inner Sanctum, The CBS Radio Mystery Hour, X-Minus One,* and *The Hermit's Cave* on my AM FM radio. These programs inspired me to create stories not just to be read, but to be listened to.

Introduction

I'll just say up front, Kevin's work is the easiest to narrate and produce of any author I've had the pleasure of working with. I can say this with some surety because, to date, his is the only work that has caused me to suffer a genuine panic attack during production. While recording my adaptation of "The Box-Born Wraith," contentedly tucked into the sweaty darkness of my ramshackle closet studio, alone, save for the emotionless glow of Adobe Audition before me, throat raw from all the guttural pigeon ghoulish required of that piece, it very suddenly dawned on me just how similar my accommodations had come to resemble those of the titular "Wraith." Staggered by the sudden invasion of art into life, my breathing became labored, and my heart began to race. Assisted by the characteristically unfortunate levels of caffeine and impending doom in my system, I threw open the door, sprinted out of the apartment, and gave the fresh evening air a few minutes to calm my nerves. Unsurprisingly, that one did not require a second take.

From a narrator's perspective, it is particularly easy to inhabit the characters from Kevin's stories because they just feel "lived in." When voicing the rough-edged truckers from "Green Eyes and Chili Dogs," or the stoic and determined family man from "Contractions," I'm sometimes reminded of the work of director John Carpenter. In Carpenter's films, especially *The Thing*, very little back-story is provided for any particular character; however, the audience is always effortlessly aware of who that person is, who that person was, and how that person fits into the social fabric of their environment with minimal, if any, exposition. In essence, and to risk a cliché, the stories read themselves. I just add sound effects.

Speaking of which, the sound-effects portion isn't exactly a struggle either. Kevin builds worlds for the mind's eye, easily painted over with audio. The damp and diseased stronghold of the ghouls, the phantasmagoric, contracting, and decrepit world in collapse, the simultaneously sinister and oh-so-lovely Halloween nights just to name a few. All these environments, exceptionally constructed to be neither too specific nor too broad, are what attracted me to narrating his work in the first place, allowing for a production distinctly my own and, hopefully, better than the other guy's.

Were I pressed to identify any one problem I have with Kevin's work, it would simply be that some of them just end too soon. That's not to say that I'd prefer his stories wrapped in a bow. A master of leaving the reader wanting more, Kevin's open endings are some of the most satisfying and least pretentious I've ever come across. Still, I and a number of enthusiastic commentators on YouTube are a little curious as to how, specifically, Benny, newly undead, will ultimately settle his debts with the mob? How did Dale and Earl get so deep into the monster-hunting game? Do the pious pacifist ghouls of "The Box-Born Wraith" get along with the cannibal farmer ghouls of "Third Shift"? Personally, I think I enjoy not knowing...sort of.

–Jason Hill

The Box-Born Wraith

"Not like this, Ciao," Benny pleaded. "Just shoot me. Please."

Ciao shook his head. "You know I can't, Ben. The Boss was very specific. Now get in the damn box."

Benny gazed at the six-foot-long wooden crate at the bottom of the shallow grave. It looked to be hurried work, all imperfect corners and protruding nails. Ciao's men weren't carpenters; they were killers. This box, with all its imperfections, buried in the middle of an old graveyard, was Benny's coffin.

He knew it was pointless to beg but didn't know what else to do. "Please, Ciao, not alive. Don't bury me alive."

"Jump down there, you skimming bastard, or I'm gonna blow your kneecaps off." Ciao aimed his gun at Benny's legs. "If you don't panic, you got about twenty-four hours of air. You want to spend that time in agony?"

Benny considered for a second, but one of Ciao's men pushed him in before he could decide. He landed on his hands and feet and stood up fast, the top of the grave coming to his chest. Benny's heart pounded, and even on this cool October night, sweat matted his black hair.

Ciao knelt. "Ya know, the Boss owns this old boneyard. Bought it a year back, when the last vacancy was filled. He thought it'd be a nice place to bury the trash. You'll be the first."

Benny looked out at the sea of gravestones jutting up from a thin layer of fog as orange moonlight shimmered off of a hundred forgotten epitaphs. The only terrestrial source of light came from the porches outside the cemetery. Jack-o'-lanterns burned brightly in the surrounding neighborhood, and as Benny was about to start begging again, he caught a glint of movement.

Ciao saw it, too, and Benny felt the revolver's muzzle pressed up to his jaw. "Go ahead, Ben, call out."

Benny gazed at the trick-or-treaters skipping along the sidewalk outside the cemetery, a small group of parents in tow.

"Make one sound and I'll blow your mouth clean off; then I'll have to go kill some kids. You don't want to go down like that, Ben, and I ain't in no mood to kill kids."

Benny opened his mouth, and Ciao leaned closer. "Then, when that is done, maybe I go pay a visit to your house, Benny-boy. Say hi to that nice wife and kid of yours. Is he out trick-or-treating tonight?"

Benny grabbed Ciao's collar. "Stay away from my family, you son-of-a-bitch."

Ciao pointed the gun into Benny's grave. "Get in the box and they'll be fine."

Benny knew far too well that Ciao didn't make threats. He made promises. The sadistic pig would have no problem abusing his family while Benny slowly suffocated. Sighing, he let his hands fall to his side and gazed down at where he was meant to die. It was cold, hard, and dark.

"Attaboy. Now lie down and let's get this done."

Benny lowered himself into the box, and the darkness swept over him like a blanket. " Ciao, let me have a light."

Ciao kicked some dirt into the grave, landing on Benny's chest. "Won't change nothin'."

4

"I don't want to die in the dark."

Ciao pulled a flashlight from his back pocket and tossed it down. "We all die in the dark, Benny."

Fumbling with the flashlight, Benny pulled it to his chest as Ciao's men threw down the lid. One of them jumped in the hole with a hammer and nails. Benny placed his hands on the lid as the goon slid it into place, then he lifted his head and peered through the cracks. Ciao stood, holstered his gun, and turned to go. "Hey, Ciao," Benny called.

"Yeah."

Benny clenched his teeth. "If I ever see you again..."

Ciao smiled. "You won't."

Benny closed his eyes as the first nail was put in place. He managed to make it through the hammering, staying calm, retreating into thoughts of his wife and son. But when the dirt fell in loud clumps, Benny started to lose control. His body shook, and he started pounding, then clawing at the lid. Wooded shards broke loose and stabbed the tender skin under his nails.

Blood ran down his fingers as the sound of falling dirt became distant, replaced by the creaking of the wooden coffin. He placed his hands flat on the lid, realizing it was bowing inward from the weight of the dirt. He started to laugh, thinking that the lid might implode and crush him. But after a few silent moments, Benny realized he wasn't going to be that lucky.

The smell of earth, sweat, and freshly cut wood filled his nostrils as he tried to take slow breaths. The sounds of his breathing bounced around the box like a trapped bat, amplifying his panic, feeding his dread.

Benny tried to occupy his mind and not think about his itching neck or his aching legs. He desperately wanted to bend his knees, just for a few seconds, and the fact that he couldn't was maddening. He screamed and pounded at the lid with his fists. Then he heard the faint sounds of someone sobbing. As he pressed his forehead to the top of the box, he realized it was him. His echoing cries continued for twenty minutes, then, energy spent, he passed out.

He awoke with a jolt and smacked his head on unforgiving wood, an instant reminder that the nightmare of being buried alive hadn't been a nightmare.

He moved the light to check his watch. Just past midnight. He'd been buried for four hours. *Twenty hours to go*, he thought. *I can do this. Just make it through the next twenty hours without losing my mind and...*

A distant sound seized his attention. Benny held his breath, straining to hear it again. He pressed his ear to the lid, and there it was again—a faint digging sound. Someone was digging. He tried to call out, "I'm in...," but his previous screams had strained his voice.

It had to be Ciao digging him up, Benny thought. Maybe the Boss just wanted to teach him a lesson. Seemed a bit extreme, but...

The digging got closer.

Or maybe it was teenagers on a dare, digging up a fresh grave. Yeah, that might be it. It's the kind of Halloween stunt he'd have pulled as a kid. Benny pounded on the lid again. "Here! I'm in here!"

But even before the echo of his voice had faded, he noticed something wrong with the sounds of dirt being moved. It was getting closer, more hurried, and seemed only a few feet away. But the closer it got, the more wrong it seemed.

It wasn't until Benny turned his head and pressed an ear to the bottom of the box that he realized what it was. The digging wasn't coming from above. It was coming from below.

"Oh, Jesus," Benny cried, gripping the flashlight and shining its beam around the box. He could feel dirt fall away beneath him, the bottom of the box sagging downward, hanging over a black hole in the earth.

Something scraped against the bottom, and Benny jumped.

He squirmed, trying to roll on his side, but before he did, something clawed its way down the length of the coffin. Benny froze. Taking a deep breath, he turned his head to the side, aiming the light at the widest seam in the box. The beam bounced off a dirt wall a few feet away, and he saw deep claw marks on its surface.

He could hear movement outside, accompanying his panicked breathing, but every time he chased it down with the flashlight, there was nothing. Then, like earthworms caressing his skin, he felt warm air on the back of his neck as something very close exhaled. Pulse pounding, he jerked around, eyes wide, and was terrified to see something from outside glaring in.

Large white eyes with thick eyelids of pale skin blinked and then narrowed curiously. Benny kicked the box. "Get away!"

He braced for another kick, but a dozen clawed hands burst through the box, seized his limbs, and pulled him, screaming, downward. His head slammed hard onto dirt as bits of wood rained down around him. He blinked a few times and got his focus, instantly wishing he hadn't.

A dozen golf ball-sized eyes, set inside hideous faces, surrounded him. Before Benny took a breath, he felt clawed hands grab his shirt. The creature pulled Benny's face in close, sniffing him through a pair of slits below its wide eyes. It howled angrily and pushed him away. Some of the other creatures moved away in revulsion; some looked angry, and one just stared, astonished.

Sitting up, Benny studied his captors. Their long arms allowed them simian-like movements, reaching forward on worn knuckles and swinging their legs underneath. If it weren't for their noseless faces and the hairless skin that hung off them like a Shar Pei, Benny would have thought them hairless chimpanzees.

A few of the creatures wore clothes, not for function, but more as decoration. He cringed in horror, recognizing several popular tattoo patterns on their garments, realizing their clothes were fashioned from human skin.

They shoved Benny toward a torch-lit corridor, and as the small group started to move, he had to stay crouched in the four-foot-high passage, which was the perfect size for its inhabitants.

Stumbling along the descending tunnel, Benny was prodded from behind with a blow every few minutes. He could hear them talking in a language he'd never heard before, but the tone was unquestionably angry.

Suddenly, he emerged into an enormous gymnasium-sized chamber. Coffins, stacked like bleachers, lined the walls. The seats were filled with females of the species and hordes of their brood. As he walked past, the smaller eyes of the young ones, glazed over with hunger, stared at him, disappointment flashing over their gaunt faces. The scene reminded Benny of pictures of starving children, their bloated stomachs ripe with malnutrition.

A tall, thin female, wearing human teeth around her neck like a pearl necklace, emerged from behind a pile of discarded jewelry, watches, and gold fillings. She walked toward Benny holding a staff constructed of bone. The others cleared a path, and Benny tried to stand up straight.

She tapped his chest with the staff and then placed a hand over his heart. Benny felt it beat faster at her touch. She shook her head, then turned to her people and spoke in their strange language.

They didn't like what she had to say. A commotion exploded around the room. Some yelled with rage, some sobbed. The one that had grabbed him earlier pushed to the front and started yelling. He held a broken femur like a dagger and thrust it up and down.

The female defiantly jabbed her staff into the dirt. The larger male took a step back with a slight bow, but then roared savagely and lunged at Benny. Benny brought his hands up as the creature landed on his chest. Swinging a fist, Benny connected with the side of its bald head. It fell back, howling like an enraged ape, then came again, this time with teeth.

Benny heard a crunch and screamed as it bit into his wrist. Feeling teeth touching bone, he knew he had only seconds before he lost his hand. He pulled with all his strength, wildly thrashing and kicking at his attacker. But the creature suddenly let go. It stumbled back, gagging, Benny's blood splattered on its face. It gasped for air, grabbed its throat, then fell to the dirt floor. Its tiny legs twitched, and then it lay still, dead.

Before Benny could check his wound, the female pulled him up, dragged him to the rear of the chamber and through an opening. Crouching, Benny whirled around and saw her wave the bone staff at the doorway. In an instant, the opening to the room vanished, replaced by a wall of dirt.

Thinking it safe for the moment, Benny examined his wrist. To his astonishment, he wasn't even bleeding. The cuts were deep, but there was no pain. It's like he was looking at a wound on someone else's body.

The female moved past him, and Benny gazed around the room, noticing the familiarity of his new surroundings in an instant. It had a high cathedral ceiling, pews made of coffins, and a podium of mud and bone. Beyond lay an altar decorated with elaborate hieroglyphs. The creatures were depicted carrying coffins, worshiping them, and feasting on the contents.

"Life," the female said. "The boxes are life."

Benny's head was spinning, but he started to understand. A word floated around in his mind for a few moments, seemingly searching for a sane place to land. When sanity seemed unavailable, he finely just said it. "Ghouls."

"Boxes empty for so long," she said, her speech labored as if struggling for every syllable. "Then you."

"You eat the dead to live," Benny said, more to himself than to his savior. Remembering what happened to the one that had just bit him, he knew why they couldn't consume him alive. Living blood was poisonous. "But why not just kill me now and eat me after?" he said. "I mean, you're ghouls."

She thrust the staff past the altar, toward a mud statue of a female, arms spread wide, reaching for the surface. "The Mother forbids. Must not make dead."

"Mother forbids," Benny repeated. "Well, don't that beat all. The ghouls got religion." He looked into her huge eyes as an idea erupted in his mind. "I think you and I can work this out." Benny pointed up. "You send me back up there, and I'll fill your boxes. Man, oh man, will I fill your boxes." Benny saw the female smile, a yellowed, jagged-tooth grin, and he knew she understood.

Benny clawed his way out of the ground through a narrow hole in the earth the female ghoul had created with a thrust of her staff. Flopping down on the cemetery grass, he drew air deep into his lungs, the cold night invigorating every muscle in his body.

He rolled over and looked at his wound. It still didn't hurt, and he'd almost forgotten about it. The wounds in the flesh seemed only scratches, and beneath he could feel the muscle pulse with energy he'd never felt before. His scalp tingled, and he ran his fingers through his hair. Thick black strands fell away. He looked at the clumps in his hands, sighing. "Small price to pay," he said with a grin. Benny took a deep breath and then jumped to his feet with a simian's grace.

He felt strong, hungry, and ready to make good on a promise. He didn't know what he was becoming, but he did know that Ciao would be the first to find out.

The **FUBAR** Ritual

"What the hell is that?" Mark said. "It's where we're going to conduct the ritual," Albert said.

Mark leaned forward in his wheelchair, pointing. "No, I mean that."

"According to my research, this symbol will bring forth the demon. The one that will do our bidding and restore your legs."

"Yeah, okay, but I think you drew the wrong symbol."

"It's right. It's a pentagram, sometimes referred to as a panicle to those in the know."

"No, it's not, you idiot. That's the Star of David. And unless the demon is Jewish, I don't think he's coming."

"Look, you put me in charge of the ritual," Albert said, "and I'm doing my best. I found this place, didn't I?"

"Yeah, about that," Mark rolled back and gestured to the structure's dilapidated roof.

"We're supposed to be in a place of darkness and death—a cemetery, slaughterhouse...the DMV—anything but an abandoned... What was this? A factory?"

Albert got to his feet. "Do you know what they used to make

here?" He gestured to the cobweb-covered equipment and conveyor belts around them, faintly visible in the light cast from Albert's lantern.

Mark shook his head. "No idea."

"This was the main factory for Anderson's Turkey Pot Pies."

Mark folded his arms. "Never heard of them."

"Neither did I. They went out of business in the eighties, but the town archives say this place was the biggest employer in the county. They made millions of pies a year."

"So?"

"So, this place, *this building,* is where millions of turkeys met their end. How's that for death and darkness?"

Mark sighed, looking unimpressed.

"Okay fine," Albert said. "Look, it's a small town, and it's all we got. Do you want to do this or not?"

Mark thought for a moment. Did he really want to do this? Regaining the use of his legs through dark magic. Seems like the kind of thing that works in the movies but not in real life. Oh well... It's not like he had anything else to do tonight in this crappy, unsympathetic town. And the worst thing that could happen is he'd wake up tomorrow, still crippled.

"Okay, what else do you got?" Mark said.

Albert smiled. "Flesh, that was once alive." Albert pulled something from his bag.

"Is that a chicken? A frozen chicken?" Albert asked.

"Look, if you're gonna nitpick everything—"

"No, no," Mark said. "Please continue."

Albert pulled out another item. "The hair of a virgin."

"Where did you get the hair?"

"My sister."

Mark laughed. "Your sister is not a..." Mark stopped himself. "Never mind, please continue."

Albert pulled out the next item. "An object of mysterious origin." He pulled away its tinfoil wrappings, revealing some-

thing that was both smooth and rough, hairy and balding, color-
ful and transparent.

"What is that?" Mark leaned forward. "It looks familiar."

"It should be," Albert said. "They served it in the cafeteria
last week with the meatless meatloaf, remember?"

"Oh, yeah," Mark said. "I heard Paul Krendler ate one on
a dare, and he hasn't been back to school since."

"Object of mysterious origin," Albert repeated, a little more
prideful this time; then he set it with the other objects. "And
last but not least... An offering from the modern world."

"Is that your little brother's phone?"

"Yeah," Albert said, turning it over and showing off the Pika-
chu protective case. "He is getting upgraded for his birthday
next week anyway, so he won't have long to miss this one. Besides, all he ever does is play *Pokemon Go*. So immature."

"You play that?"

"No," Albert said. "Not really. A bit. On the weekends. If I
have time— Are you ready to get this party started?"

"Absolutely. Let's go. What do I do?"

Albert tossed him a lighter. "Start lighting the candles."

There were at least twenty candles arranged in a circle
around the pentagram and/or Star of David, which had a diameter of about six feet. It was obvious that Albert had swiped his
little sister's sidewalk chalk because the six-pointed star was
purple. And the candles Mark was lighting were leftover birthday candles, the kind you find in a junk drawer, half-used and
fashioned to represent various themes of birthdays past. Pirate
candles, *Star Wars, Dora the Explorer, Curious George*, dinosaurs, and quite a few that were just numbers, a half-melted number eight, nine, and two ones. With neither of them having jobs,
the budget for the dark magic ritual was on the low side, but this
was starting to feel ridiculous. He couldn't imagine what kind
of demon would show up with these crappy offerings.

Oh, well, this was all just make-believe anyway. And in

some ways, it was as much for Albert as it was for Mark. Albert harbored guilt for Mark's condition. Mark had known that for a while, but they'd never talked about it. What was the point? It had been Albert's idea to build the go-cart when they were nine, and it had been Albert's idea to test it on Forman's Hill. And it had been Albert who had chickened out at the last moment, leaving Mark to pilot the cart down the hill alone. Albert wasn't responsible for putting the enormous oak in Mark's way, the one he cracked his head on and broke his back. But he did push him off, running along the side, his legs pumping like pistons, and just before he let go, he said, "See you on the other side."

Mark never asked Albert what he had meant by that. He'd even forgotten about it with all that had happened after hitting the tree. Physical therapy, learning to live in half of a body, and adjusting every vision he'd ever had about his future took up most of his time. It wasn't until recently that he remembered those words. Why, he couldn't say.

Mark lit the last candle and looked over at Albert. "What're you doing?"

"I'm outlining the whole area in salt. We stay on the outside, and the demon is stuck on the inside."

"What's that smell?"

"Lavender, I think."

"Bath salt?"

"Yeah. My mom has bags of this stuff."

The purplish salt went with the pretty purple chalked star, which Mark wanted to comment on, but then thought better of it. "Where do you want me?"

"Set yourself at the bottom of the pentagram, outside the salt line, and make sure you're out of reach."

"How far can a demon reach?"

Albert stopped pouring salt. "Ah, I didn't see..." He glanced over at the papers he printed out from the internet. "...Not sure—"

"Wasn't a real question," Mark said, rolling into position. "I'll just eyeball it."

Finishing the bath salt circle, Albert tossed the bag to the side and then picked up his short stack of papers. He flipped through them, then seemed to find his place. "Okay, we need to picture a door. Both of us. Hold the image in our minds."

"What kind of door?" Mark said.

"I don't know. Just a door."

"Well, like a single door? A double door? Does it have a screen or one of those little windows or peepholes?"

Albert flipped through his pages. "It can be any kind of door. We just have to picture the same door. What was the first door you thought of?"

"Honestly?"

"Yeah."

"Your sister's."

"What?"

"Well, remember before she painted it all black, it had that rainbow pattern with flowers and the *My Little Pony* stickers."

"Why the hell would you think of that?"

"I always thought it was so cool. My parents would never let me do that to my door."

"Fine," Albert said. "We'll both think of that. Which version, all black or *My Little Pony*?"

"Ponies."

Albert frowned. "I'm sensing that you're not taking this seriously."

Mark chuckled. "Dude, I just lit *Star Wars* and *Curious George* candles to summon a demon."

"Hey, I went to a lot of trouble to set this up."

Mark grimaced. "Dude, *Curious George* candles?"

"Okay," Albert said. "I went to a moderate amount of trouble to set this up."

Mark didn't respond, just stared back at his friend.

"Yeah, okay, I half-assed some of this, but this stuff is just symbols. Superficial offerings." He held out the papers. "It's these incantations that are the real magic, and according to EnterTheDarkness.com, this will work."

"Well, if it's on the internet, it must be real," Mark said. "What's next?"

Albert turned off the lantern. Although there were almost twenty candles, they didn't put out anywhere near as much light as the lantern had. Darkness within the abandoned factory grew closer, and Mark couldn't see very much beyond their circle. The conveyor belts and static equipment were just strange shapes in the encroaching blackness.

Albert sat opposite Mark. He crossed his legs and met his friend's eyes. "Are you visualizing the door?"

Mark nodded. "Ponies and all."

"Then let's begin." Albert held out the papers. "*Krappa zet-touw bowl Kerpla. Estra mine furkrepta.*"

"What language is that?"

"I don't know."

"Sounds like Klingon."

"It's not Klingon."

"How do you know you're even pronouncing it right?"

"Phonetic spelling was provided with the text, and there's a How-To video on YouTube. Any more questions?"

"No, I'm good. Sorry. Picturing the door."

"*Sebatwo, sebatwo, frakka kronin pickle. Tittlepow whichen--camp the fenny go men ra—*"

Several candles flared a bit, as if a small cloud of methane had passed near. Mark's heart quickened, and he gazed across the circle. Mark saw his own surprise mixed with excitement mirrored on Albert's face. "Keep going."

"Uhm," Albert searched for his place. "*Ramen koodle ba sum treka mir fenni auf, fenni lu, fenni bop un can, fenni amadeus.*"

"Is that it?"

"No, there's like a whole page I have to do."

"Why did you stop?"

"Well, I...I just noticed something."

Before Mark could ask what, he noticed it as well. The center of the star was gone. He could still see the chalk outline all right, but in the center section, where once there was an old, scuffed cement floor, there was now no floor at all, and in its place, a hole. "When did that happen?"

Albert shook his head. He motioned to the papers in his hand with a tilt of his head.

Mark nodded enthusiastically, then took a deep breath in an attempt to quell his shaking hands. When that didn't work, he gripped the arms of his chair tight.

"*Fenni abdual es son, fenni maklin kendow...*"

As Albert continued his recitation, Mark couldn't take his eyes off the hole in the cement floor. *Is it an optical illusion? No. It's real.* The candles shed no light into the opening, but somehow Mark knew that even if he'd shown a flashlight down into it, its depths would remain unseen.

The whole idea that there was a hole in the middle of the floor, appearing from nowhere, was disturbing on several levels. *Where did it come from? What was down there? How far to the bottom? And what was going to come through?* But even more mind-blowing, something was happening. *Really* happening. Albert's shitty household offerings and internet magic spell were actually working.

Mark felt himself roll back a few inches. Albert stopped reading again, and the two stared at one another. Then Mark rolled again. He reached down and locked his wheels, and that is when he realized why he'd been rolling. The floor was tilting. Not a lot. Just a little, like a slight flutter of a seesaw.

"Keep going," Mark said.

"Almost done."

Mark felt a little nauseated and looked out into the factory to steady himself. He'd always been prone to motion sickness, even before the accident. He needed to lock his eyes on a fixed object in the distance. The faint outlines of the conveyor belts would do, but he couldn't find them. Not the belts or the equipment. Gone. Beyond the candlelight that reached about fifteen feet around the circle, he could only see darkness. No shapes of any kind. Just black.

His stomach tightened, and it felt as if he'd swallowed a handful of nails. And though he knew in every fiber of his being that it could not be true, he could not help the feeling that they were not in the factory anymore.

He looked over at Albert, who seemed to be finishing up. "...*twana kalpindrew, fenni ma, fenni tru, fenni nicto, und I be estralenny, no fenni, no fenni, no fenni more.*"

"Now what?"

Albert shrugged. "I guess—"

A clanking sound rose from the hole. Old chains clinking, turning, twisting. Then a rhythmic clicking like something turning on a pully, slow, steady. The sound grew louder. Mark imaged something being hoisted upward on thick chains. The sounds grew loud as if whatever was making them had risen from the hole and was right in front of them. But they saw nothing.

Then, after excruciatingly long seconds, movement. Staring into the hole, Mark's mouth fell open as something large rose from the darkness. Hoisted up into the air by unseen chains, it rose before them. Something rectangular, something thin, something...pink.

"Your sister's door," Mark said as it rose above them. The clanking sounds stopped, and the door, gold hinges fastened to a purple frame and all, dangled ten feet in the air, hovering over the star.

Mark felt dizzy and realized he wasn't breathing. He took two fast breaths, and before he exhaled the second one, Albert was at his side.

"Thought you might be lonely over here by yourself."

Mark nodded. "Good call."

They looked up at the door, hanging above them like some strange piece of modern art that neither one of them knew what to do with.

Far in the distance, there was a sound like someone falling down stairs, rolling, fighting against the fall, pausing for a second, then tumbling again. Then something hit the door with a powerful *thud*.

"What the hell?" a deep voice said from the other side of the door. "Ah, you gotta be kidding me."

"Hello," Mark said. "Are you all right?"

"Who said that?" returned the voice. The door handle started to wiggle, like someone trying to figure out how it worked. Before Mark could answer, the door flew open. He caught sight of a very surprised face as it fell forward, screaming, "Holy shhhhh..."

Mark watched in horror as a body tumbled through the door, landing with a splat. It lay very still for several moments. Mark reached out, wanting to help, but Albert grabbed his arm and shook his head. Mark sat back in his chair. "Are you hurt?"

"Ahhh," the demon said. Sprawled out and naked, it slowly drew its limbs in toward its body like a scared child huddled on the cold floor. Its legs were shriveled twigs and didn't look as if they functioned. Gray skin wrapped loosely around its bent bones and gaunt legs. The toenails hadn't been cut in a century, and its left arm was in the same condition. The right arm was another matter. It looked like the arm of a bodybuilder, ripped with muscle, almost cartoonishly so, and its skin glistened with a healthy flesh tone. So different from everything else on the demon, it was easy to imagine it originating from an entirely different body.

Struggling, it lifted its bald, wrinkled head, eyes fluttering, one green, one scarlet. "Where am I?"

"Indiana," Albert said. "We summoned you."

The demon flipped onto its belly and used its muscled arm to rise, resting on a pointed elbow. "Summoned me? You can't summon me."

"Why not?" Mark said.

"I did my time in the human world. It chewed me up and spit me out," it said, spittle coming from its gray lips. "I'm retired."

Albert leaned over and whispered to Mark. "I read about this. It said he would say anything to get out of doing what we ask. Try to trick us, lie."

"We don't believe you," Mark said. "You have been summoned and must obey."

The demon chuckled. "You must have screwed it up really good if you got me here. Is that a frozen chicken?"

"It's almost thawed," Albert countered.

With its one good arm, the demon pulled itself forward to the edge of the purple salt and sniffed. "Lavender?"

"It's my mom's favorite."

"Very nice," the demon said and rolled onto its back. "One moment I'm having a martini in my condo with a beautiful view of the river Styx, the next I'm... Why is the door all the way up there? I almost broke my neck."

"Sorry," Albert said. "It's our first time using black magic, or any magic, really."

"You don't say," the demon said, rolling back onto his belly, the lower half of his body flopping uselessly. "Listen here, kids, this isn't amateur hour. You have summoned a demon. Not a high demon, or even a very powerful one, but a demon nonetheless. In my day, I might have been able to do something for you, or I might have just eaten your faces; either way, we would have moved forward. But read my lips: I. Am. Retired. So send me back and we'll forget about your little trip down Daigon Alley, you'll get to keep your faces, and I can get back to my martini."

"No," Albert said. "You can return to your domain when you have granted our request."

"Okay, this is the last time I'm going to put it nicely. You have screwed this up. Your offerings are insulting at best, and your...am I...am I lying on a Star of David?"

"Yeah," Albert said. "It might be."

"Jesus Christ," the demon said. "Whatever it is, although I can make an educated guess—" The demon looked at Mark's chair and then continued. "—you're not going to get it. Send me back."

Mark felt a surge of anger. It was as if all the doctors he'd seen in the past eight years with their lack of encouragement, depressing diagnosis, and their just-learn-to-live-with-it attitude were fueling his temper. For years he'd wanted to scream almost every day, scream at the doctors, his over-concerned parents, his teachers with their unwanted pity, at everyone in this stupid, little town. Even at Albert, with his two perfectly healthy legs. And here was a chance to undo all that. Make everything go away. Hit the reset button, and this thing, this shriveled little creature with the power to fix him, was saying no.

"You're not going anywhere," Mark said. "You have been summoned, and you will grant our request."

"Have it your way, kids," the demon said. "But since your offerings are dismal—and I suspect your reading of the unholy words were equally appalling—there must be a sacrifice."

"What?" Albert said. "No, there is nothing in my research that said we needed to make a sacrifice once we have you here. The offerings should be enough."

"How did you come by your research?" the demon asked.

"Google," Albert said.

The demon rolled his different colored eyes. "Check the fine print of your instructions—paragraph six, subsection six, line six; you can read it for yourself."

Albert skimmed through his handful of papers, flipping to almost the last page. "Oh, crap."

"What?"

"He's telling the truth."

"What does it say?"

"If the offerings are deemed subpar and or there are errors in the reading of the unholy words, then a sacrifice must be made in order to proceed. One human soul per request. The more significant the sacrifice to the one making the request, the more potent will be the magic used."

"Which means, Mark..." The demon smiled. "...the more important the soul is to you, the more powerful the magic I can use to grant your request. Still want to play this game, kids?"

"I swear I didn't know about this," Albert said. "What do you want to do?"

"What will happen to our sacrifice?" Mark said.

"If you are even considering going forward with this," the demon said, "then you really don't want to know."

"Shit," Albert said. "That doesn't sound good. Let's pick someone we hate."

"Do you two idiots understand the meaning of sacrifice? Sending someone you hate into the darkness isn't a sacrifice. It's a favor, one you would owe for. If you want this to work, it must be someone you care about. Love, even. The stronger your feelings, the greater your chance of getting what you want. I cannot be any clearer than that."

Albert leaned close to Mark and lowered his voice. "How about Paul Krendler?"

"If he did eat the mysterious object served in the cafeteria, then he's dead already. Even if he isn't, I don't have any feelings... I mean, I don't care about him," Mark whispered.

"How about Mary Feng? You've been crushing on her since eighth grade?"

"No," Mark said too loud, then lowered his voice back to a whisper. "She's the one I want to ask to the prom. I've been dreaming of dancing with her the moment I get my legs back."

"If you don't get your legs back, you won't be dancing with

anyone at the prom."

"I guess," Mark said, wondering if he could really do it. Then he had a thought. Maybe there was a better choice. Someone that would be a real sacrifice. Someone that he had cared about since kindergarten, someone who had cared about him. And someone who was partially responsible for him being in this wheelchair in the first place. But could he do it?

"So, Mary then?" Albert whispered.

Mark nodded.

"Has a choice been made?" the demon said.

"Yes," Mark said.

"Do not speak the name aloud; hold it in your mind," the demon said. "The magic will be more powerful."

Mark was relieved about that. He didn't know if he could go through with it otherwise.

"What's next," Albert said.

"Your request," the demon said. "Again, do not speak it aloud. I must take it from you."

The demon closed his eyes, and Mark could feel him entering his memories, like someone flipping through folders in a file cabinet."

"That little town of yours, Bunker Hill, has made you feel like an outcast," the demon said.

"Yes," Mark said.

"Bullies call you Wheels, Halfling, and Roller Boy."

Mark nodded, his eyes glassy.

"You couldn't go on the field trip last week because of the hiking and the stairs to the lookout. Many places that everyone else can go are off-limits to you," the demon said.

"Yes," Mark said.

"You want to go anywhere they can go."

"Yes."

"You want your legs to work just as well as everyone else's in that shithole you call a town," the demon said. "I understand."

"Yes."

"It is time; go through the door."

"What door?" Albert said.

The demon pointed a finger to their left. The pink door with its purple frame was now resting on the ground ten feet away, at the edge of where the candlelight faded into darkness.

"Go through it now!"

Mark felt the urgency in the demon's voice deep in his chest. His heart thumped like a jackhammer. He unlocked his wheels, spun to the left, and headed for the door.

"Wait," Albert said.

Mark didn't want to look back. He reached the door and grabbed the handle.

"Wait, Mark," Albert pleaded. "I can't move."

Mark turned the handle.

"Why can't I move?"

The door opened, and Mark hesitated. He looked back. Albert was still in the position he'd left him, crouched next to a chair that was no longer there. The demon's enormous hand, muscles pulsing, reached out beyond the circle. Its fingers enveloped Albert's ankle.

"No," Albert screamed.

"Go now," the demon shouted, "or his sacrifice will be for nothing."

"I'm sorry, Albert," Mark said, though not loud enough for anyone to hear.

Mark turned back to the door. A scream boomed behind him as he propelled himself through the pink and purple opening. Before he passed completely through its frame, he felt himself falling. His chair fell away, and he watched it tumble into a void of swirling color. There was an explosion of fire. He felt the heat before he saw the flames, rising from beneath him. The flames consumed him in an instant, and everything burned. Even his legs were on fire. He felt them burn.

Mark sat up in his bed, covered in sweat. He ran his hands over his body, quickly checking for flames. He wasn't on fire. He wasn't even warm. "What the hell," he said to an empty bedroom. He couldn't remember how he'd gotten home or putting on his pajamas. *Did it really happen?*

Although the flames were not real, the pain he felt certainly was. Even the pain in his legs. Real pain. In his legs. He pulled the blankets away and looked at his useless limbs. They didn't look different. He touched them with both hands. No feeling. Nothing.

A stupid dream. Just stupid, wishful dreaming.

He wiped his eyes and ran his fingers through his hair. If disappointment were a sledgehammer, it would have cracked his skull open. The worst of it was that he now had to summon the energy to get up and be the town's crippled boy again, as he was yesterday and the day before.

Soft sobbing filtered into his room. Familiar. He looked at his slightly ajar door. The weeping got louder, then a *thud* came from down the hall.

"Mom!" Mark yelled.

There was uncontrollable crying coming from somewhere in his house.

Mark reached for his chair. "Mom, are you all right?"

His mom responded, but through the crying, he could not understand what she said.

"Dad," Mark yelled. "What's wrong with mom?"

A helicopter buzzed the house as Mark's dad yelled back from down the hall. "I don't know, son. We can't... Are you okay?"

"I'm fine. Why is mom crying?"

"Just stay there," Mark's dad said. "Everything is gonna be all right. Everything..."

"Dad!"

Mark lunged for his chair. It was a bit out of reach, but he managed. He slid in his seat and moved to the hall. His heart was racing, his fingers trembling, and his grip on his handrims was shaky, barely enough to propel him. He leaned forward, hoping the chair would follow. The sound of his mother's tears was maddening. *Was she hurt? Was someone hurting her? And why had dad stopped talking?*

"Mom, I'm coming," Mark shouted, barreling toward his bedroom door. He had navigated the opening to his room hundreds—no, thousands of times—but in his desperation to reach his mother, his aim was off. Not a lot, but enough to hang his left rear wheel on the doorframe. His chair tilted one way, and Mark tumbled the other.

He hit the floor with a solid smack, a stomach-punching belly flop. He looked back at the empty chair, almost with a look of betrayal. Instantly he realized he could crawl to his parent's room in half the time it would take to remount his chair. With the wind knocked out of him and his ribs bruised, he pulled himself forward.

"Dad," Mark shouted, rising on his hands.

The lack of response sent a wave of fear through his body. He hand-walked the next few yards in seconds. The door to the master bedroom was ajar, and with no concern how it would feel, he hit the door with his forehead, sending it wide open. "Mom!"

He first saw her face, one middle-aged cheek pressed to the carpet. Then her outstretched hands, fingernails digging into the shag. One leg was on the floor, half under the bed; the other was trapped midway between the floor and the bed, hung up in the bedding.

"Mom," Mark hurried over to her and took her hand. "What's wrong?"

"I...I can't move," she said, tears running into the carpet.

Mark rose and scanned the bed, catching sight of his father, sitting up, hands over his face. "Dad, Mom fell," Mark said. "Please, come help her."

His father dropped his hands, looked at his son with glassy eyes, and said, "I can't."

"This can't be right," said Bill Hollowell, weekend anchor at CNN.

"Just read the statement, Bill," the news director said through Bill's earpiece. "We're gonna skip the usual intro and go right into it."

"But John, is this true?"

"We have no way of verifying it, but it is an official statement. We'll cut to Jill on location after you read the release. You can throw some questions her way...you're live in five, four..."

Bill watched the opening graphics scroll across the monitor, and before he was ready, the stage manager pointed at him.

He swallowed hard before speaking. "After a forty-eight-hour quarantine of the entire town of Bunker Hill, Indiana, the CDC, in collaboration with the World Health Organization, has finally released a statement." Bill waited a beat for the text to appear on the monitor. "On the morning of June sixth, an unknown pathogen affected the residents of Bunker Hill, Indiana. The situation is town-wide, and the CDC, with the assistance of the National Guard, has taken these extreme quarantine measures to ensure the safety of the surrounding counties and the general population at large. The origins of this disease, its gestation period, and how it is transmitted have all yet to be identified, but the main symptom is consistent with all infected. Every resident who was physically in the town of Bunker Hill at six a.m. on the morning of June sixth is experiencing paralysis from the waist down. Every man, woman, and child has become paralyzed."

Liberation

To most people, it was just an ordinary Thursday, but to Caroline, today was the day she decided to rid herself of the spiders living in her brain. Even though they pulled only a single spider from that woman in Brazil, there had to be more than one in her brain, living just under the skullcap like lizards burrowed beneath the floorboards.

It had to be more than one. Caroline had so much passion and determination when she was young; it would take several brain-dwelling parasites to eat it all. The spiders lived off the brain impulses of her desire, feeding on her resolve to do the things she really wanted to do. "That's what the spiders live on," Caroline had said to her roommate exactly one week ago.

From her favorite chair in their small living room, Wendy shook her head. "Please tell me you're joking, Caroline."

Stepping toward Wendy, Caroline's intensity grew. "It's all right here." She held out the medical journal, dated July 1986, and pointed to a picture of a woman lying unconscious in an archaic-looking operating room. Then she slid her finger across to a murky photo on the opposite page, something hideously pale, swollen. The photograph was slightly out of focus, like all the images ever captured of Bigfoot and the Loch Ness Monster, but a multi-legged form was discernable.

It had the characteristics of a spider but looked more like some underwater creature—a mutated octopus or alien squid. The arachnid's legs were thick, like tentacles, and splayed out on a porcelain table. Pools of blood spotted the off-white surface, and a pair of forceps lay next to the spider, providing a sense of scale. The creature's creamy white frame looked to be about four inches in length. The image reminded Caroline of salamanders discovered deep in subterranean caves. Living their whole lives in darkness, the creatures appeared pasty—sickly.

Leaning in, Wendy traced a finger along the picture's caption. "It says it didn't have any eyes."

"It doesn't need them," Caroline said, grinning. "It lives in darkness, feeling its way around." Just like the salamanders.

Wendy stood up. "This doesn't prove anything, Caroline. You don't have spiders living in your brain, for God's sake." She put a hand on her hip, sighing deeply. "Okay, let's be logical about this for a second. That woman, whoever the hell she is, lives in Brazil. And I'll admit there are all kinds of freaky shit living in the rainforest that we don't know about yet, but spiders that eat your determination, turning women into breeder cows? Come on! And even if there were, how did they get to Seattle? I don't remember you vacationing in Brazil recently, or ever."

Caroline had anticipated this question because it had occurred to her as well. She had never been out of the state of Washington in her life, let alone south of the equator. She had always wanted to travel. Paris, Rome, Vienna. But when it came down to it, her resolve to make the arrangements seemed to evaporate. Damn spiders!

Caroline slapped the journal closed. "I didn't need to go to Brazil. The spiders were brought to me."

Wendy raised a brow. "What?"

"The rainforest has been harvested and exported for our consumption since the fifties."

"What are you talking about?"

"Where do you think most of our medicines come from? Our birth control, Prozac, Valium? Hell, even our makeup, moisturizers, eyeliner, and lipstick. You name it. It all comes from the rainforest. Women have been inundated with this stuff for more than fifty years."

"Jeez, you've given this a lot of thought."

"Is it so hard to believe that these parasites could have hitched a ride in our birth control pills or some hair product packaged by men for women?"

Wendy sighed and held out a hand. "Look, I know you've gone through some rough shit. That asshole husband of yours getting custody of your kids—God, I don't know how I could live with that. But it doesn't mean there's anything wrong with you." Wendy stepped forward, her green eyes empathetic. "You've got your life on track now. In a few months, we'll both pass our exams and be certified RNs. It's gonna be—"

"I don't even want to be a nurse," Caroline snapped. "That's what I'm talking about. It was my husband's decision. He made all the arrangements. Where we would live. When we would have kids. What kind of career I should have. Why I needed to get a second job to pay for his education. Who he would fuck behind my back."

Caroline pictured the unwanted events in her life. "Through everything, I never objected. Didn't complain, not once. My existence is like a movie I'm watching. I didn't want to have kids. I don't think I even wanted to get married. All my life I've wanted to do things. But I've never done them. Not one."

When Caroline looked up again, she noticed that Wendy had backed away.

"Don't you see?" Caroline gestured to herself. "It's not just me. Why do you think women are second-class citizens? Why do we accept lower pay for the same job done by a man?" Caroline pointed at Wendy. "Why do you sleep with all those guys when you said you really didn't want to?"

Wendy's eyes flashed with anger. "There are no spiders living in our brains, goddamn it. I can't believe I'm even having this conversion."

"That's what they want you to believe."

"The spiders?"

Caroline nodded. "And men."

Wendy quieted for a moment, seeming deep in thought. She blinked and then looked at Caroline. "I've put up with all your craziness, but this... I can't be here right now." She hurried toward the front door of their small high-rise apartment. "Being your friend is just too hard. I'm gonna... I'm gonna just go."

Caroline rushed after her, catching the door as Wendy opened it. "You don't really want to go. It's the spid—"

"Let go of the fucking door," Wendy said, harsh words soaked in fear.

Caroline felt like she'd been doused with a bucket of cold water. She let go of the door.

Wendy moved through the opening, and without looking back, she said, "Get some help, Caroline. Seriously."

Caroline slammed the door.

That was a week ago, and Caroline hadn't seen her since. Two days later, Wendy returned to the apartment to get her belongings while Caroline was on duty at the hospital. She must have been in a hurry because she left a couple of things. Knick-knacks mostly, some cookware. Even the note she wrote echoing her final words to Caroline seemed rushed.

Get some help. Please.

Placing the stainless steel bit of the cranial drill on the bathroom counter, Caroline surveyed the instruments of her liberation. Scalpel, forceps, sutures, and gauze, all laid out according to size on the countertop. After a moment's pause, it suddenly struck her funny that the countertop resembled the chalky por-celain table in the medical journal photo of the Brazilian brain spider.

She almost laughed but stopped herself—the sutures above her hipbone were still very tender. She had performed a prelimi-nary procedure on herself earlier in the morning, extracting the few ounces of fat she'd need later to plug the hole.

She picked up the forceps and turned them over in her hand. If she used too much pressure, she might tear the legs off, al-lowing the spider to scurry to the safety and darkness of her gray matter. Need a soft touch. Her surgical instructor had said the same thing moments before the first brain surgery she had assisted with. The patient, some man, died on the table, but not before Caroline got an excellent crash course in poking around the human brain.

She set the forceps next to the Tupperware container holding her body fat. She pinned back her auburn hair, exposing the pale patch of scalp she had shaved clean, just an inch above her ear. It glistened with a single bead of sweat in the soft glow of the bathroom light. She tapped the shaved area with her finger.

Numb.

She had only injected herself with a third of the recommend-ed dose of anesthetic for such a procedure—one requiring the patient to remain conscious. A full dose might have made it dif-ficult to stand or keep a clear head. In any case, her partial dose meant there would be some pain. How much?

Putting her hands on the counter, she stared at her small frame in the mirror. She wore only underwear and an Alanis Morissette concert t-shirt. She hadn't actually gone to the con-cert. She'd wanted to but didn't.

The bathroom window behind her was reflected in the mir-ror. Its curtain was open, and the Seattle skyline bled through. The Space Needle was as erect as ever, jutting up from a pubic layer of fog, reminding her who really ran the world.

She wanted privacy, so she turned and drew the curtain. Liberation was often a lone pursuit.

Days before, she began picturing how she would do this. Do it quickly. Do it fast. Don't think about it. Thinking might let the spiders know you're coming.

She picked up the scalpel and touched it to her numbed flesh. She had planned to cut a fast x-shaped incision, but when she pulled back the blade, the wound looked more like a bleeding cross.

She dabbed with the gauze until the blood flow subsided, then wiped away the sweat from her brow. Using the scalpel, she cut deeper and then peeled back the folds of flesh, exposing her skull. Not much, just enough to touch the drill bit to bone.

No pain yet.

She lifted the drill and inserted the bit in the breach on her scalp. When the stainless steel point touched her skull, she felt the contact all the way down her spine. The sensation reverberated through her limbs, tapering off like ripples on a liquid surface.

She breathed fast, forcing the air in and out. Her heart raced. She pressed her lips together and gritted her teeth.

Very soon now, she told herself. Liberation.

The sound of the drill coming to life startled her, but not enough to lose focus. She gently pushed the drill inward, keeping her hand steady. Thin bands of smoke laced with ground bone fragments drifted up from the point of contact. *Perfectly normal*, she told herself. *Doing fine.*

The drill went deeper, and she kept a close watch on the depth, trying to avoid piercing the meninges completely—the three layers of membranes protecting the brain. She was amazed at the lack of pain, but as the familiar burning smell reached her nostrils, blinding white light exploded in her skull.

Agony pulsed like a camera flash going off in her brain. Each flash caused her knees to buckle a little more. She closed her eyes and screamed, reaching for the mirror. *Open your eyes, goddamn it, open your eyes. Fight through this.*

She opened one eye and then the other. The drill bit wasn't moving. Her finger had come off the button. *Damn it.* But as she pushed the bit forward, she realized nothing solid was pushing back. She had broken through. She backed the drill out of the hole she'd made and then unfolded the surgical mirror rigged to the medicine cabinet.

A clear, yellow-tinted liquid was dripping from the hole. *Oh, shit.* Cerebrospinal fluid. She had broken through the middle meninge layer—the arachnoid. Images from her textbooks depicted this area as a cobweb of thread-like strands attaching to the innermost region. It was where the spiders lived. But the appearance of cerebrospinal fluid meant she had gone below this into the subarachnoid layer. There was only a finite amount of this precious fluid protecting her brain. Losing a little was okay; most people did throughout their lifetime. But losing a lot was deadly.

She tilted her head to keep the fluid from spilling out. She picked up a penlight, clicked it on, then aimed the beam into her exposed brain. The fluid seemed to be stabilizing. *Thank God.*

Her pain had tapered off, except in regions completely foreign to where all the action was. The muscles around her ribs ached enormously, and pulsing pains anchored themselves in the soles of her feet.

She took a deep breath and switched the penlight on and off, aiming the flickering beam into the hole in her skull. Up until this point, her plan contained elements of familiar territory. As a surgical RN, she had assisted many similar procedures on dozens of patients. But the next part of her plan was sheer guesswork.

She hoped that the brain spiders had evolved like other creatures that inhabited the dark. Bottom-dwelling enigmas living in the deepest ocean trenches shared a fascination with the eyeless subterranean salamanders. Although none needed light to survive, they would be drawn to it by an instinctual curiosity. Even the creatures without eyes turned toward the light, like a blind man sensing the exact moment someone else entered the room.

Caroline's thumb ached as she flicked the light on and off. Rotating the penlight in her hand, she tried using her index finger to press the button but found it difficult to aim the light. Then it occurred to Caroline that she could leave the light on and wave it back and forth over the hole. From the spider's point of view, it would look the same. Why didn't these things occur to her sooner? Maybe the spiders feed on common sense as well. That would explain a lot.

Minutes went by. She started to feel dizzy. I can't do this much longer. "Come out, come out, wherever you are."

Suddenly, there was movement. Subtle at first. Probing. Just an ivory tip. Then, a white needle-like leg emerged.

Caroline stopped moving the penlight and held her breath.

The thin pasty leg explored the lit area like a blind person's cane. Then it abruptly stopped. Motionless. It was as if it had suddenly become aware it was being watched.

Caroline reached down for the forceps. Her hand fell on the empty counter. She wanted to look down at the countertop for the instrument but was afraid to take her eyes off the tiny leg's reflection in the mirror. If she looked away, it might disappear. She locked her gaze on the arachnid, willing it to stay.

She felt along the counter as the spider's leg investigated the jagged edges of the freshly cut bone. Another leg appeared. Then another.

Caroline's fingers grazed the forceps handle. *Thank God.* She lifted them and opened the needle-nose end. She eased the instrument forward, watching her movements in the surgical mirror.

Three legs, almost an inch long, protruded from her skull.

Each one seemed determined to explore a different area of her scalp.

The open forceps hovered over the thickest point of two legs, and Caroline swallowed hard. She felt six years old again, playing that silly game, Operation. The similarities were uncanny. Use your tweezers to remove the ghost-white plastic bones without touching the metal edge. A steady hand wins the game, but graze the edge and you lose your turn.

More was at stake than losing a turn. If the spider broke free or she tore its legs off, she would lose her one chance to regain her will. Her life.

She clamped the forceps around the spidery appendages and, using a touch so soft and accurate she could have picked up a grain of rice, she began to pull.

The spider didn't come at first. Several other legs appeared, and it looked like they were searching for a way to anchor themselves. Then it began to slip. It slid quickly through the hole like a newborn calf being born. Caroline flicked it into the sink, unclamping the forceps. She glanced down at it, but there was new movement in the mirror.

A second spider had found its way to the hole, its legs probing at the light. *How many*, she wondered. *How many?*

Ten minutes later, she had her answer. There were three in all. The third seemed to climb through the hole of its own volition, needing very little encouragement from the forceps. Maybe the spiders sought a kind of liberation of their own.

She repaired the meninges and packed the hole in her skull with her own body fat. This should have been surprisingly painful, but it wasn't. She knew that the body's pain receptors could turn themselves off in extreme conditions, but she didn't think that was what was happening. As she sutured her scalp, she glanced at her body in the mirror. She remembered it being so small before, dwarfed in the ceiling-to-countertop glass. But now it looked as if the mirror could barely contain her frame.

She felt different. She was different.

Liberated.

The last suture tied, she clipped the excess stitching away. As she laid down the scissors, exhaustion hit her. She bent forward, bracing herself on the counter. Her head hung over the sink, hair dangling above the porcelain. She drew slow, deep breaths and took her first opportunity to examine the parasites. She blinked a few times, not immediately registering what was wrong.

Gone.

The sink was empty.

She smiled as she pictured the watery arachnids scurrying down the drain, traversing the miles of plumbing under the city. *Liberation, my friends. Liberation.*

The air in the bathroom smelled foul. She staggered to the window. She wanted to draw the curtain open, but she ended up pulling it off the rod. Pressing her forehead to the glass, she looked down at the women scurrying on the streets that spun out like a web from downtown. *So many women,* she told herself. *There are more of us than there are men.* She felt troubled watching women rushing to jobs they didn't want, raising families they didn't want—hell, even wearing shoes they didn't want.

There're so many of us. So many women in need of liberation. I'm gonna need a lot more drill bits.

There was a tapping at the bathroom door. "Hey, Caroline. It's me, Wendy. I know I should have called before coming over like this."

Caroline pushed away from the window.

"Especially after how I left and all. I'm sorry about that. Anyway, I just wanted to come by and pick up my pots and pans. I met this guy, and he wants me to cook my famous Italian casserole for him tonight. I know, I know, I hate to cook, but I really like this guy."

Caroline moved over to the counter.

Wendy rapped on the door again. "Are you in there?"

Caroline grinned at her tall and free-willed image in the mirror. She picked up the drill.

Time to start the liberation.

Momentum

The world wasn't ending quickly like a well-placed shotgun blast in the mouth, but rather like Dwight always figured it would—twisting and squirming, sucking in every last foul breath, hoping for just one more shot at life. Dwight knew his time was limited, but he was making an all-American effort to see how long he could last. Not out of any survivalist mentality. It was more plain, old-fashioned curiosity. He wanted to hang on 'til the end to see how the world finally blinked out. Would there be a bang or just a pathetic whimper?

Even after it hit the fan out there, Dwight never ventured far from the carnival grounds. His fellow carnies had all left in search of family members to spend their final moments with. But Dwight's family was still here. The decaying façade of the carnival—its dust-covered rides, the derelict concessions, and the rigged carney games—were the only family he needed.

The gaming area, where beaus emptied their wallets trying to win a poorly stitched teddy bear for their wide-eyed gals— was where Dwight had spent most of his adult life. So why should he leave simply because the world was ending?

By the time the girl had wandered into the carnival, Dwight could hardly remember how many weeks it had been since the world lost power. Had it been weeks? A month maybe? The girl limped over to a bench next to his venue—the Strongman game.

He had been watching her for a while. She staggered, fell, pushed herself up, then collapsed onto a wooden bench, its paint peeling in handfuls from the chemicals and unnatural compounds that had rained down from space—an event that CNN had christened "The Last Catastrophe."

He waited until she sat up before he approached. She looked like she had been startled enough, so he approached carefully.

She did not raise her head as he neared. He purposely shuffled his feet, attempting to capture her attention, but her gaze remained downcast.

Perhaps she had fallen asleep. He stood waiting at the tip of her shadow. Her body wasn't in great shape, but whose was these days? At least she still looked human. Mostly. Her clothes were threadbare, only enough left to cover the areas demanding concealment in the former modest world.

"Hey, you alive?" Dwight said.

Her head shot up with a start, eyes wide. It seemed for a moment like she was going to flee. Her arms rose and then collapsed into her lap. Her terrified expression melted into a kind of acceptance, and she sighed.

Dwight did his best to appear non-threatening. "Now, I ain't that ugly, is I?" He smiled, showing a few missing teeth. In a world where most were losing teeth, hair, and the proper use of their limbs as appendages mutated into something less human-looking, Dwight felt pretty darn good about his appearance. End of the world or not, the bar on the scale of attractiveness had been lowered considerably.

"Bet you think it's all 'bout strength," Dwight said.

She managed to raise an eyebrow. "What..."

Dwight pointed to the Strongman game, where an oversized sledgehammer leaned against the launcher. "Smacking that bell between the lady's honkers." At the top of the game's pole, some twenty feet above the ground, was a painting of a woman, her breasts thrust forward and the bell just covering the nipples. "It's not about strength, ya know." Dwight got down on one knee like a man about to propose. "It's all about momentum. I know. I used to work this game. You know, when things weren't so...different."

The hint of a smile flickered in her eyes.

"What did you used to do? You know, before."

She grinned as if what she was about to say was funny. "I was a mortgage analyst for a title company."

Dwight ran his fingers through his greasy hair. "No idea what that is. Guess it doesn't matter now, do it?"

She shook her head.

"I'm Dwight."

"Carrie."

"Nice to meet you, Carrie."

"I don't mean to..." She leaned forward. "Do you have any food?"

Dwight looked around as if searching for listening ears, then said, "Not on me. But I got a place under the Fun House. Ain't much."

"Could you go get the food and bring it here?"

"Don't trust me, huh? Hell, I don't blame ya. God only knows whatcha been through. What we all been through."

She sat back on the bench, averting her gaze.

"Look, it's not safe to bring food out here, and besides, it'll be dark soon. You know what that means, dontcha?"

Carrie nodded slowly, seeming to relive some horrific memory.

Dwight slapped his hands together and got to his feet. "Tell ya what, Carrie. If I can ring that bell three times using only one arm, will ya come back with me?"

She looked up at him. "I'm sure you can. You used to work

41

here."

Dwight walked to the game and picked up the sledgehammer. "Okay, you caught me trying to be sly. But I can't pass up the chance to show off for a lady." He held the hammer out as if asking permission.

She smiled and blushed. "Well, go ahead."

With one hand, Dwight started swinging the sledgehammer around in big, over-the-shoulder circles, each revolution building in momentum until, finally, he brought the hammer down on the launcher, right on the sweet spot. The shot rocketed up and smacked the bell with a clang. "Like I said, nothing to do with strength." He repeated the action and rang the bell again.

By the time the clang of the third ring had faded, Carrie was clapping, but not hard enough to make any sound.

Dwight dropped the hammer and held out his hand. "It's all about momentum. Now we best get a move on, 'cause that bell tends to attract the ones that slither, and a couple of them suckers are awful fast."

She nodded and took his hand. He pulled her up, amazed at how light she was. Couldn't have been a hundred pounds. She walked most of the way but needed to grab hold of his shoulders as they descended the stairs in the Fun House. Dwight sealed the door behind them and then stuffed towels around the cracks of the door. The night wanderers had an acute sense of smell, and more than once, they'd stumbled down the stairs, following the aroma of Dwight's flesh.

When Dwight finished, Carrie looked around, candlelight flickering in her eyes.

Dwight reached for one of the middle-sized sledgehammers he had begun polishing just after the world started to go. He propped it on his shoulder.

"There is no food down here," Carrie said.

"There is now." Dwight swung the hammer. It connected with the side of her head right on the sweet spot. Like a twig giving way to a heavy boot heel, her neck snapped cleanly.

Her lifeless form stood there for a beat, a marionette in the moment after its strings had been cut. Then it slumped to the floor.

Dwight held up the business end of the sledgehammer in his right hand, amazed at how little blood spotted its surface. He felt it was because he didn't bludgeon his food like some wild animal. He swung the hammer artfully—a master of momentum.

Babysitting for Writers

"The kids are fine, Mister Brandner," Mindy said into the phone. *Not that Mister Big-Time Writer had bothered to ask.*

The voice on the line sounded winded. "That's great... Mindy. Just...please—"

"Are you jogging or something?" Mindy twirled a blonde strand around her finger.

"No, running. But never...mind. I really need you to do me a favor."

Here we go again. Jeez, wasn't it enough that she came early, helped his spoiled kids carve their jack-o'-lanterns, and took them trick-or-treating. *Totally above and beyond the call.* Now there were going to be more extracurricular babysitting duties, like last week when he called right in the middle of the *Vampire Diaries* and asked her to thumb through some amazingly dull, pictureless book in his study just to read a footnote.

Gawd! I hate babysitting for writers.

Mindy popped her gum. "I'm kinda busy right now." She

glanced over at her two young charges, passed out on the sofa, their Halloween-candy sugar rush having finally given out. "Your kids want me to read them a story."

"Mindy, this is important."

It's always important. "Fine. What do you need?"

"Go to the study. I need you to find something."

Instinctively, Mindy was already heading in that direction. She stepped through the large cherry wood doorframe marking the study's entrance. "I'm here," Mindy said with zero enthusiasm. "What am I looking for?"

"On the desk there...is a stack of files."

She glared at the huge desk covered with papers, a pile of file folders, several stacks of very uninteresting-looking books, and a knife sheathed in leather. "Yep."

"The one I need should be near...the top."

Mindy picked one off the pile and decided then and there that she was not babysitting for this guy anymore. She isn't like... secretary-girl.

Turning the folder sideways, she read the name aloud. "Voodoo and Santa...Santeria. What's Santa—"

"Not that one. Go to the next."

Mindy grabbed another. "Egyptian, Book of the Dead."

"No! Next one."

She didn't like his tone. "Mister Brandner, I'm not paid enough to get yelled at." The fact was, he paid her more than enough to get yelled at, but she didn't have to like it.

"Sorry... Please try again, Mindy."

"Fine." She picked up the knife, which sat on another smaller pile of files, then set it on a shelf with other knives, swords, and strange-looking implements she didn't have names for. Sighing, she grabbed the file on top of the small pile and read, "Werewolves in America."

"That's it!" Static popped on the line, making his next few words impossible to understand.

"Mister Brandner, maybe you should stop jogging," Mindy suggested. "It's getting really hard to understand you."

"Not...an option at the moment. Just open that file and look for a highlighted paragraph. There'll be...handwritten notes in the...margin. Should say, reverse incantation, and how...to kill."

Popping her gum loudly into the phone, she started flipping through the pages, scanning, getting more bored by the second.

"Find it?"

Jeez, patients much? "Still looking." Mindy hoped this wasn't going to take much longer. Her boyfriend was on his way over, and after they tucked the brats in their beds, they were gonna— "Here it is," Mindy said.

Mr. Brandner didn't respond.

"Hey, I found it. Helloooo."

Mindy heard him breathing hard, then a tumbling *thud*, as if he'd tripped.

"Hello, Mister Brandner."

The phone connection started to crackle. Mindy thought she heard him say something, but it sounded more like a growl. Then the line went dead.

How rude, Mindy scoffed. That'll teach him to jog and talk on the phone. *Who does that?* Oh, well. If it was important, he'd call back. He always did.

Blood, Gridlock, and PEZ

I hate birthdays. Not other people's, just mine.

The universe, with its transcendent sense of humor, seems to gather up a year's worth of misery, and then, on my birthday, it delivers the whole painful lot in one big, annual cosmic joke that I never seem to get. On my seventh birthday, my dog was not just killed but dragged under a car for almost half a mile, ki-yiing the entire time. Our house burned to the ground on my tenth birthday, and on my eleventh, my dad split from my mom, leaving her with a black eye.

My sixteenth birthday is the day I received my first sexual advance. A pretty momentous day for most, but not when it comes from your uncle. I rejected his incestuous advance by throwing up on him. Family holidays were never quite the same after that.

But believe it or not, one birthday trumps them all, the chiseled images of which no amount of therapy could erase from my memory. On my eighteenth birthday, I found myself sitting on the highway next to a corpse.

Blood gathered in pools around the body as the afternoon sun gave it a sickly glimmer. I remember thinking how much the dark liquid seemed to belong on the pavement. Like oil, transmission fluid, or lizard-green coolant, the blood was at home on the asphalt.

It's amazing what you notice when events force you to grow up in the span of a moment. But I'm getting ahead of myself. This story really starts two hours earlier, with Gina.

"What the hell?" Gina sat in the passenger seat of my 2004 Mazda sedan. We both gawked, open-mouthed, at the distant flames licking the sky about a half-mile ahead of us.

The car accident that had turned all five lanes of the Interstate into a massive parking lot had apparently become more serious. Even in the daylight, the soft glow from the fire cast an orange luster on my windshield. A thick mushroom of black smoke rose from the carnage, then bled into the afternoon sky.

"No way that can be good," I said as the whine of emergency vehicles sounded in the distance.

I glanced around at the surrounding vehicles. Most of the drivers had turned off their engines. Every few minutes, a highway patrol car, paramedic, or ambulance sped past along the shoulder, but other than that, nothing moved.

"Jesus, Craig, we're never going to get there," Gina said. "How long have we been stuck here?"

"'Bout twenty minutes," I said.

"Ahhhrr, feels like forever. Why can't they just move the bodies to the side of the road and open up a couple of lanes?"

I always knew Gina was insensitive, but it was a rare occasion when it took voice.

"Christ, Gina. People are probably dying up there."

"Well, I'm dying here," Gina snapped. "And I have to pee."

I reached over and held out my half-empty Big Gulp. "One container. No waiting."

She looked at me as if I had just tossed dog shit on her shoes. "Have you ever had a straw shoved up your nose?"

"That's why I love you, Gina," I said. "All that sweet pillow talk."

"Go suck an elf." She folded her arms.

A groggy voice floated up from behind us. "Are we there yet?" Pitt, my best friend, was waking up in the backseat. It had been Pitt's idea to go to the L.A. Toy Convention—just a few hours' drive from our hometown of Delano, California. Knowing my luck with birthdays, Pitt wanted us to get out of town, reasoning that if anything bad were going to happen, at least we would be near the beach.

I looked at him in the rearview mirror, and before Gina or I answered, Pitt's eyes flickered like dying light bulbs, then winked out as he fell back asleep.

Growing up together, Pitt and I had developed the same fondness for toys, comic books, video games, and all other things that anchored us solidly in the harbor of our youth. Our hobbies didn't exactly endear us to the opposite sex, but they helped forge a bond between us. A bond I thought couldn't be broken. Then came Gina.

"Shit, he can sleep through anything," Gina said.

"How would you know what he can sleep through?"

Gina flicked her hair and dealt me a steely, green-eyed glare. "What the hell is that supposed to mean?"

I had been rehearsing my response to such a remark for two weeks. I started working on it about the time I caught Pitt and Gina together at school. Nothing was incriminating about their manner; it was simply the fact that they were together. Until then, I was under the impression that they didn't much like each other's company and only endured it on occasion for my benefit. Whenever he could, Pitt told me what a bitch she was, and Gina never missed an opportunity to call Pitt a loser.

Seeing them together just didn't fit. Unless I was missing

something.

The opportunity for accusation had arrived, but as I opened my mouth to speak, a car horn started beeping. The intensity of my gaze should have transfixed Gina, but the odd blaring of the horn stole her attention.

She looked back over at Pitt and then out the back window. "I think someone's car alarm is going off."

"Why would someone turn on a car alarm in a traffic jam?"

"I don't know... There. Two cars back. Do you see him?" Gina pointed.

I reluctantly turned around. I saw nothing at first. But then the strangeness of the scene drew my gaze like lightning to a rod. Two cars back and one lane over was a man ramming his forehead repeatedly into his steering wheel.

"There's something you don't see every day," I said.

"He's gone crazy." Gina was a big fan of stating the obvious.

"Well, he is driving an El Camino. That's never been the trademark of sanity."

The man using his car horn as a percussion instrument stopped abruptly and sat up. Then he began speaking or possibly yelling. We couldn't hear anything, but he looked like an actor in a silent movie—exaggerating the pronunciation of whatever it was he was saying.

"What do you think is wrong with him?" Gina said.

"I don't know or care. Maybe he has to pee."

Gina turned back to me. "Look, Craig, do you have something to say? Seriously, 'cause this dancing around crap is getting old."

My moment was gone, and my courage left me like helium escaping a ruptured balloon. She was now the aggressor, and I no longer felt accusatory, no matter what Gina and Pitt were doing behind my back.

I sank into my seat and reached into my shirt pocket. I retrieved a collectible Dumbo PEZ dispenser, one of the many toys we all collected. I quickly dispensed a grape candy and popped it into my mouth, then held the dispenser out to her.

"PEZ?"

It was the perfect peace offering. We had met in an online PEZ forum. Our conversation quickly moved into a private chat room, where we discussed all the finer points of stem colors. If I knew Gina, she'd think the gesture romantic.

Her mouth relaxed, her luscious pink lips smiling. A silent moment passed as her features softened, and she again resembled the girl I had fallen in love with. Just for a moment, I was taken back. Could I fix this?

She accepted a candy and held it to her mouth, then gestured to the dispenser. "Doesn't that belong to Pitt?"

"Yeah," I said, taking a deep breath. "I took it from him when he fell asleep. I'm holding it hostage until he kicks in for gas. Tired of him freeloading."

I could tell she wanted to say something in Pitt's defense, but she hesitated and pursed her lips.

That's when I knew. Gina and Pitt were together. And this was not fixable.

"Do you have something you want to tell me?" I wasn't sure if I wanted to hear the answer.

Her lower lip quivered. I thought for a moment she might produce a tear, but she suddenly looked out the back window. "What is he doing now?"

"Who?"

"That guy." She pointed over Pitt's sleeping head.

My gaze followed, once again finding the man in the El Camino. He was now slamming his head against the driver's side window and still mouthing some unheard silver-screen monologue.

"Jeez," I said. "Somebody get a net."

Gina shifted in her seat. "He needs to switch to decaf." She started to laugh, then abruptly looked down at her seatbelt.

"Damn!"

"What?"

"This belt hates me. It unbuckles whenever it wants to and sticks when I want out." She tried buckling it, but it wouldn't catch.

"At our current speed, I think you're pretty safe."

"Just help me," she said. "Why don't you get this damn thing fixed?"

I reached over and grabbed the buckle. "It's a bit tricky. You have to hold the button down and click it in before you release..."

Our hands touched, and she immediately pulled away. Her reaction felt like a knife turning in my gut.

Happy birthday to me.

I finished securing her belt, then faced forward. With my hands on the dashboard, I rested my head on the steering wheel. I wondered if Mr. El Camino got any kind of satisfaction by slamming his head into the horn.

"I know you don't love me anymore," I said.

Gina let silence speak for her as she sat forward in her seat.

"But... do you even like me?" I felt her hand on my shoulder, and I tensed up, waiting for her to speak, but the next voice I heard wasn't Gina's. It was Pitt's.

"Do you guys know there's a guy back here slamming his head against his window?"

"Yes," Gina snapped.

"Why do you think he's doing that?" Pitt said.

"Why would anybody do that? Craig thinks he has to pee."

"Wow!" Pitt said.

Gina turned to look back. "What?"

"He just broke the window with his head," Pitt said.

I turned around. The man in the El Camino was bleeding from his forehead.

"Maybe someone should go see if he's all right," I said.

"Are you nuts?" Gina's gaze met mine.

"I didn't mean somebody us. I mean somebody else." It came out harsher than I had intended.

Pitt must have detected something in my voice because he turned toward Gina and me with a confused look. "Okay, what'd I miss?"

"Shut up, Pitt, just shut up," Gina said.

"Yep. Definitely missed something." Pitt slumped into the backseat.

Gina leaned into my personal space. "Let's just have a nice day. We've been looking forward to this for months. When we get back..." She didn't finish. Maybe it was the first time she was going to say it out loud, or maybe she didn't want Pitt to know how she was going to phrase it. Hell, I didn't want to know how she was going to phrase it.

I looked back at Pitt. He seemed to be catching up to what was going on, and I could tell he wished his dance with the Sandman hadn't ended when it did. He folded his arms across his chest.

He may have been preparing to say something, but the look of growing horror on my face as I looked past him out the window must have given him pause.

"Christ," I said. Gina and Pitt both turned around to follow my gaze.

Mr. El Camino had gotten out of his car. He stood next to his open door, his right foot tapping the white line that divided the lanes. His hair was dark and disobedient in all directions, except where blood had matted it to his scalp.

His eyes were so wide open that they looked like huge, white spheres that would've been more at home on a cartoon character. When he took a step forward, it was awkward and jerky, like the darting movements of the Keystone Cops in a Max Sennett silent comedy. I would have expected Buster Keaton or the great Charley Chaplin to join him on screen if it hadn't been for the enormous ax he gripped in both hands.

The dried blood caked on the stainless steel blade and his now-audible ranting shattered any illusion that what I was watching was a classic from the golden age of silent film.

I don't recall the rest of that afternoon as a continuous stream of events, complete with living characters moving from scene to scene in cinematic transition. It's more like still images in a slideshow I'd rather not watch. I have a mental picture of him leaning down and peering into the passenger window of the vehicle next to his El Camino. He screamed at the glass, leaving speckles of saliva on the window.

The woman on the other side of the glass was trying to ignore him. Sitting in the front passenger seat of an all-terrain vehicle, she turned her head away and continued talking to the man in the driver's seat. The driver was also doing his best not to make eye contact with the screaming maniac. They both seemed to come from a place where the credo is: *If you don't look at crazy people, they'll just go away.*

I have to believe that the couple would have reacted differently had they been able to see the ax. Mr. El Camino held it slightly behind him, and from the couple's point of view, his presence was merely an annoyance. Like a homeless guy threatening to clean their windshield with a soiled newspaper.

But we saw it, and the twenty or so people looking on from various vehicles saw it. We all saw it. And we simply did nothing.

Paralyzed with some sick fascination for impending violence, everyone peered out like patrons at a drive-in waiting for the horror movie to move beyond the opening credits. I guess it hadn't occurred to anyone to venture outside and offer assistance or, at the very least, yell a warning to the couple.

Perhaps we all harbored the same childish illusion—the illusion of safety you feel when tucked comfortably in a car with the windows rolled up. Like kids hiding under the covers to ward off the closet monster.

Without warning or hesitation, Mr. El Comino reared back, the ax held high, and brought it down on the windshield. This first blow demolished the glass. The second blow did the same to the woman's face.

"Holy sh—did you see that?" Pitt said.

"It's time to leave," I said. Dozens of people around us came to the same conclusion.

I opened my door and stuck out my foot. The passenger fleeing the Chevy truck in the next lane flung his door open. Our doors collided, sending mine back, closing on my leg. The pain was crushing, and I felt it in my teeth.

A herd of people rushed by, and leading the pack was Pitt. He must have escaped through one of the rear doors.

When there was a break in the stream of panic, I pushed the door open again, stepping out on my injured leg. I immediately turned back, half expecting to see the business end of the ax, too close to fend off.

What I saw instead was the man climbing from his SUV and making his way around to confront Mr. El Camino. Or maybe he was trying to help his passenger, now hemorrhaging in long, red streams from what was once an attractive face. When he got there—

Wait.

The next few moments are bathed in images I don't wish to remember, so let's fast forward past the next few and pick up the action as Mr. El Camino wrenches his ax from the man's lifeless chest.

"My portfolio is diverse—*cha-ching, cha-ching*! You must diversify!" Mr. El Camino screamed.

I am at best paraphrasing the dialogue of Pitt, Gina, and myself, as years and drink have eroded the day's surplus details. But no paraphrasing of Mr. El Camino's words will ever be necessary. Each one has a permanent, almost reverent, place in my recall, like a chiseled epitaph on a family gravestone. They are always with me.

"When you don't diversify, you get screwed—*cha-ching!*" Mr. El Camino continued as he brought the blunt end of the ax down like a sledgehammer on the windshield of his own car.

Limping southbound, I saw Pitt standing about twenty yards ahead on the left side of the road. He hadn't completely abandoned me, but he wasn't coming back for me either. I started scanning for Gina. She could run faster than both of us, and I figured she was a quarter mile away by now. When I reached Pitt, I kept searching. Didn't see her on the left shoulder.

"Are you okay?" Pitt sounded concerned.

"Yeah, I'm good. Where's Gina?" I gazed across the highway to the other side. She wasn't there either.

"Don't know. Thought she was with you."

I took a deep breath. "Figured you both would be up ahead of..." And that's when it dawned on me. I had seen Pitt get out of the car, but not Gina. My stomach seized as I turned around. "Oh, God."

Back in the car, she was tugging frantically at her seatbelt. Couple of real heroes we were.

"She can't get the buckle unlatched," I said. "Come on." I motioned for Pitt to follow me. But he wouldn't move a step. His jaw quivered, and his eyes were frozen in an unblinking gape.

I wanted to give him the benefit of the doubt. Maybe he just didn't hear me. "Pitt, come on."

Pitt shook his head slowly, eyes still unblinking.

Son-of-a-bitch.

So, there I was, about to rush back toward an ax-wielding maniac to save my soon-to-be ex-girlfriend, who had been banging my best friend. If I were successful in this venture, the one most likely to benefit would be Pitt, the same asshole who wouldn't even take a step in her direction.

I turned away, disgusted, and started my journey back toward Gina. If ever there was a bigger schmuck than me, surely his eighteenth birthday wasn't this crappy.

By this time, Mr. El Camino had finished demolishing the glass in his car and looked ready to move on. He staggered toward an abandoned Toyota just behind my car. If he spent the same amount of time smashing the Toyota's windows, I had less than a minute before he would move forward again and notice Gina.

If I stayed low and quiet, Mr. El Camino might not observe my approach. I could slip Gina out of the car, and we could get away before Mr. El Camino finished with the Toyota. When I was just a few car lengths away, Gina looked up and saw me. "Craig! Help! I can't get—" I held my finger to my lips as I ran, but Mr. El Camino spun on his heel, glaring in Gina's direction. He yanked the ax from the Toyota's windshield, showering safety glass onto the asphalt. So much for my plan.

"My credit is spotless. Run it; you'll see—*cha-ching*." He stalked toward my car, glass crackling under his boots. When he reached the passenger window, he leaned over and peered in.

Gina brought her hands up to fend off the man's gaze.

He said, "You cost me my line of credit, you bitch! It's not nice to mess with a man's livelihood." He brought the ax up to his shoulder like a baseball player taking a batter's stance.

Then he swung and smashed the side window. My heart sank as Gina's lifeless form filled my imagination.

But Gina's head popped into view, still intact. She had ducked under the dashboard, narrowly missing the ax, and now squirmed to avoid the blade again as Mr. El Camino pulled it from the car. The maniac reared back, weapon held high for another blow. I didn't think Gina could dodge another swing, so I executed the first idea that popped into my head—get his attention.

"Hey, asshole!" I yanked the Dumbo PEZ dispenser from my shirt pocket and threw it at him.

Pitt and I had been throwing PEZ dispensers at each other since we were eight. With a fully loaded dispenser, we had the accuracy of South African Bushmen hurling spears.

It tumbled through the air, head over end, Dumbo's ears providing the perfect counterbalance to its bright blue stem. Mr. El Camino looked up just in time for Dumbo to hit him square in the forehead.

The mental slide I have of this scene reminds me of a cel from a cartoon—that moment when Elmer Fudd with a shotgun in hand finally notices that wascally wabbit, Bugs Bunny.

"Do you know what it takes to build a well-diversified port-folio? *Cha-ching, cha-ching.*" Mr. El Camino stepped toward me.

I stopped about six feet from him, a distance I hoped was out of ax range. "N-no," I stammered. "Not really."

"I have perfect credit." He pointed to himself and took an-other step. "I have Diner's Club and a Platinum Card—*cha-ching.*"

"That's pretty sweet."

"But they say I'm spent." He took another step. Sweat and blood were dripping from his scalp.

"Who says?"

"They cancel my card the same day they send me an appli-cation for a new one—*cha-ching*—that says I'm pre-approved!" Spray from his saliva fell just short of my shoes. I was definitely within ax range.

"That's a real bitch," I said, taking a step back.

"I have perfect credit." He gripped the ax handle with both hands. His knuckles turned white, and his whole body started to quiver like a volcano just moments away from an eruption.

I started to take another step back. "Look, I think..."

Mr. El Camino reared up with the ax. In that split second before he swung, two choices flashed in my mind—move forward or move back? Mystifying to me even today, I rushed forward and reached for the ax handle as he swung.

My left hand missed, but my right caught it firmly. I tried to twist the weapon away, but he brought the butt of the handle up fast, catching my chin. I staggered back, collapsing onto the hood of a station wagon. I was dazed but still had enough sense to move as the ax blade smashed down next to me, slicing into the metal.

I tumbled to the asphalt, sprawling between the station wagon's bumper and the ass end of a box truck. I glimpsed the flash of metal in my peripheral vision and ducked. The ax slashed through the air above my head and thudded into the wooden roll-away door of the box truck. El Camino ripped the ax violently out of the door, sending wooden shards and dust into my face. He brought the ax up again, but I rolled under the bumper of the truck, hoping it was wide enough to offer protection.

The blade crashed down on the metal bumper. Sparks flew overhead like fireworks.

He raised the ax again. My feet were only inches from his leg. I kicked at his knee hard, connecting squarely. In action films, I had seen this move send bad guys tumbling to the ground a dozen times, allowing Bruce Willis or Jackie Chan those precious moments they needed to regain their feet and take control of the situation.

Mr. El Camino hadn't seen any of those movies.

He paused for a moment, resting the ax on his shoulder. He glanced down at his knee. At least my Nancy-boy kick had registered with him. Not the result I was going for, but I did gain a moment. I was about to scurry under the truck for cover but caught sight of someone's feet moving behind Mr. El Camino.

Those checkerboard Keds were Gina's. She must have solved her seatbelt problem and was moving in to help me. I could see her tiptoeing behind the maniac, and I wondered what her plan could be. There were a few heavy objects in my car she could use to smash him on the head: full cans of Red Bull, my grand-dad's wrench, even a brick I used when parking on a hill. All I had to do was keep this guy's attention until she could finish sneaking up behind him.

But as she moved away instead of toward me, I got a sinking feeling.

Son-of-a-chicken-shit-bitch.

I gazed up at Mr. El Camino. His head tilted, eyes narrowing, and I imagined him saying, "Hey, remember me?"

The ax came off his shoulder, and for an instant, I entertained the idea of not dodging the blow. Just let the finely crafted blade split my skull open and avoid months of pain and self-pity. A birthday present to me wrapped up and delivered by an ax-wielding nut-job.

But in that insane and chaotic moment, one in which I could have gone either way, live or die, words of wisdom filtered down from an unlikely source. Mr. El Camino.

"Women can diminish a man's financial stability. It's economic castration, *cha-ching*."

I had no idea what that meant. But somehow his words spoke to me. It's like when Frank Sinatra starts doing that *do-bee, do-wa* stuff. Nobody knows what the hell he's saying, but everybody seems to get it.

El Camino swung the ax.

And I ducked.

The blade crashed into the steel bumper again, sending more sparks flying. He reared back for another assault and swung at a lower angle, this time targeting my flailing legs.

I drew up my feet and curled into a fetal position, banging my knees on the truck's undercarriage. The blade clipped the bottom of my shoes, then punctured the frayed sidewall of the truck's rear tire. There was a great explosion of air that pelted my cheek with rubber. It stung like a bitch, but I ignored it and squirmed farther under the truck.

El Camino didn't seem fazed by the explosion. He pulled the ax from the tire and took another swing. It was a wild effort, and it went wide, gouging the asphalt next to my hip.

"High-return stocks can be elusive," he said as he crouched down. I had managed to scoot my entire body under the truck, safe from further swings. I hoped he would move on to more easily dispatchable victims.

He reached under the truck and clawed at my feet. I kicked him and moved away, my forehead scraping on the grimy muffler.

"I am not over my limit," he said, seizing my shoe.

He yanked me toward him, but I kicked off the shoe. His free hand grasped my other ankle, and his grip tightened. I started sliding across the pavement and looked around for something to grab. Anything!

I caught the rear axle, which, to my surprise, is one of the greasiest things you can grab under a vehicle. Really should have taken auto shop in high school. My hands slid down the slimy shaft as Mr. El Camino dragged me out with ease.

Once he had pulled me back into the afternoon sun, he dropped my feet. Then he moved to pick up his ax. I sat up fast, feeling dizzy. Up to this point, my life consisted of sitting on the couch playing video games, shopping for PEZ dispensers on E-bay, and sexting Gina. Besides the occasional roll in the hay with my soon-to-be ex-girlfriend, I engaged in little physical activity. If this adrenaline-induced madness didn't end soon, I was gonna puke.

El Camino turned toward me again. He raised the ax slowly over his head, preparing a straight-on, split-me-down-the-middle blow to end this cartoon. *Th-th-th-th-That's all, Folks!*

I sat there, breathing heavily, my heart pounding in my temples. I tried to move, but exhaustion prevented me. I threw my hands up and yelled, "Wait!"

El Camino tilted his head like a confused dog. The ax hung in the air, ready to descend and take my life, but for a moment, he stood still like some murderous statue sculpted just for me.

The next words from my mouth needed to be brilliant. They

had to traverse the abyss of madness and somehow carry him over to the side of sanity—where people thought it unreasonable to slaughter folks on a highway with an ax.

I said in a trembling voice, "It's my birthday."

Mr. El Camino processed these words. His head bobbed, and one eye twitched. It was like watching a broken machine, wheels and gears grinding away, but unable to complete their tasks.

His head suddenly became still, and for an instant, he looked like a man who had just returned from a long and relaxing trip. His mouth opened slowly. I prepared myself for more of his financial nonsense, but his next words were wholly and utterly sane.

"Happy birthday," he said.

It was the only birthday wish I would get all day.

I looked at his face and then the ax. "Thank you."

El Camino took a long breath, and as he exhaled, he became insane again—eyes wide, a murderous grin beneath his blood-spotted cheeks. He raised the ax toward the sun.

I wanted to dodge the blow. I knew I was going to try, but I also knew my body was done. I held my breath and waited.

Then I heard two distinct pops, like distant firecrackers going off in succession. I was marginally aware of small impacts on the truck behind me but had no idea what they could be until the crimson holes in the front of El Camino's shirt started to thicken with blood. His blood.

Mr. El Camino dropped to his knees. Behind him stood the youngest highway patrol officer I had ever seen. He didn't look old enough to go to his high school prom, let alone hold a 9-millimeter pistol, gray smoke drifting from the muzzle.

If I live a hundred years, I swear I'll never utter the phrase, *Where is a cop when you need one?*

The officer might have said something, but an explosion of pain in my left foot kept me from registering it. Mr. El Camino had let the ax slip from his hands. The blunt end landed so hard that it separated the sole of my shoe from the canvas. Even in death, El Camino was still swinging.

Two hours later, a paramedic determined, much to my surprise, that my foot was unbroken. Hospital X-rays backed up his on-the-scene assessment, but I think they all missed something. Every once in a while, even years later, I'll feel an unyielding urge to limp. I imagine a small, permanent fracture deep inside the bone—so deep X-rays can't detect it. Maybe they aren't meant to.

After the paramedics released me, I hobbled over to the shoulder where Mr. El Camino lay quietly under a yellow tarp. I sat down next to the body as if we were old friends, and in a way, we were. To paraphrase Oscar Wilde, at least this friend tried to stab me in the front.

Although my birthday had been rough, Mr. El Camino's day had been a bit worse. The evening news would report that Mr. Alec (El Camino) Harrison, an airline mechanic at Fresno International, had become widowed by his own hand. Earlier that morning he had chopped his wife into a dozen pieces, then tenderly boxed up each part and gift-wrapped them. He deposited the packages in the night drop boxes at several local banks. The news made no mention of Mr. Harrison's financial situation. On the day he died, he had just turned forty-six.

Happy birthday.

"The girl in the ambulance says this belongs to you." The young officer who had saved my life held out the Dumbo PEZ dispenser. Up close, he didn't look as young as when I first laid eyes on him, but he could still pass for a high school senior in a *21 Jump Street* kind of way.

"Thanks," I said, taking the toy from him.

"If the paramedics are done with you, my Sergeant wants to get your statement." He pointed to a burly cop standing behind the ambulance. I could see Pitt in the back with Gina, who was having her head looked at. Her hair was full of glass, and she had a few cuts on her scalp, but nothing serious.

"I'll be there in a minute," I said. The officer nodded, then turned on his heel, leaving me to my thoughts.

Later that evening, Gina's father picked her up at the hospital. Other than video news coverage, I never saw her again. About six months ago, she sent me a text. I stared at the message for a long time but never responded. Didn't see any point.

I'm not sure how long she and Pitt lasted after that day. Pitt never talked about it, and I sure as hell wasn't going to ask. Keeping in touch grew harder after graduation. My childhood friend still sends me an email now and again from whatever part of the world he's in. Last I heard, he was diving with sharks off the Australian coast—the latest daredevil stunt, much like his base jump off the Effie Tower. There is a video of it on YouTube, but I never looked.

I'm not sure what he's chasing with all these idiotic escapades. Maybe it's courage. Maybe it's something else.

As for me, I never attempted another trip to the L.A. Toy Convention. After that day, I was kind of done with toys, comic books, and video games. I never realized how much money I'd been pissing away on all that crap until I stopped. Nowadays, my funds are well managed in a very versatile portfolio with stocks, CDs, and even a bit of real estate. You see, the key to a really well-built portfolio is diversification.

Cha-ching, cha-ching.

Third Shift

Alan Carver heard the phone ring in the outer waiting room. He drummed his fingers on his old desk while listening to Helen, his assistant of thirteen years, answer the phone.

"Good evening, TM Labor," she said with a raspy voice into the antique rotary phone. Carver was hoping to get through the whole night crisis-free, but as he eavesdropped on the conversation, he realized that hope was about to be dashed. Within a minute, Helen's cigarette-scarred voice piped in through Carver's intercom.

"Alan, irate customer on line one."

Carver rolled his eyes. "Helen, we only have the one line."

"Think positive; in a year or two, we could have ten lines," she replied with her we-are-going-to-be-huge sarcasm.

"That stopped being funny about ten years ago."

"So shoot me; I love the classics."

"How irate, on a scale of one to ten?" Carver hoped for a number between four and five.

"'Bout a fifteen."

"Lovely. What's he complaining about?"

"I'd tell you in his words, but my parents didn't raise me to use that kind of language."

"Okay," Carver sighed. "Give me about thirty seconds." After a brief consideration, he added, "Then bring me a scotch."

"Your wish is my command, master." Helen signed off with a static pop.

Alan Carver, TM Labor's District Manager for West Coast Operations for over fifteen years, rolled up his sleeves and got comfortable in his leather chair. Before he was ready, line one rang. Reaching for the receiver, he glanced at the clock. It was a few ticks before midnight.

He answered the phone in his best customer-service voice. "Hello, this is Alan Carver, Third Shift Manager."

"Mister Carver, what the hell kind of service are you running?"

"I'm not sure what you're referring to, Sir," Carver replied.

"Your laborers should've started work hours ago."

Carver tried to take control of the conversation. "Let's back up a bit; tell me who you are and what property you represent."

"Oh great, I have to tell the story over again? Didn't that idiot who answered the phone tell you any of it?"

"We're not going to accomplish anything with insults, Sir. Please just tell me who you are and give me your account number if you have it."

There was a pause while Carver imagined the man composing himself. "My name is David McFarland. I don't have my account number on me. I own the McFarland Winery in Napa Valley."

"How long have you been a client of TM, Mister McFarland?"

"This is my third week."

Helen walked in with a scotch in one hand.

Pulling the receiver away from his ear, Carver spoke in a more urgent tone to his assistant. "I need a customer file on a McFarland Winery. In Napa Valley."

"I was about to go on break."

"What do I pay you for?" Carver snapped.

Helen put her hands on her hips. "The worst coffee you have ever tasted, frighteningly good looks, and mind-bending conversation."

Carver gave Helen an impatient glare.

"All right, all right," she shrugged. "I'll look for the file." After she handed him the glass, she moved to a file cabinet that looked as if it was a relic from the 1800s.

"Mister Carver, are you there?" the voice boomed on the other side of line one.

"Yes, I'm here. I was just looking for your file. Now, what can I help you with? Is the service not what we promised?"

"No, the service so far has been excellent," McFarland replied in a grudging tone.

"Then what seems to be the problem?"

"There's no one in my vineyard! I can see the field your organization is supposed to work tonight from my bedroom window. I couldn't sleep, so I thought I'd look out on the laborers you are supposed to have in my field, starting at ten p.m. It's almost midnight, so where are they?"

"Okay," Carver said. "This is a common misunderstanding with our service. Our laborers do eight hours of work in less than four hours. We meet the negotiated shift quota in half the time, so our workers don't show up until midnight and will be gone by four a.m." He took a quick sip of scotch. "I'm assuming they've been meeting their quotas for grapes picked, Mister McFarland?"

"Yes, they have. Even exceeded it a few times. But why not just have them work the full eight hours of third shift? I could use the boost in production."

"We can't do that, Mister McFarland. We need a buffer of at least two hours between the end of your second shift and the beginning of your first shift so that our laborers on third don't run into any of your people. Your Sales Rep must have explained this to you."

"Look, I don't care if you're using illegals to work my field. Do I sound like I'm from immigration? I just want to know, when are they going to start work?"

"As I said, they will work your field from twelve a.m. to four a.m., and they'll be gone by the time your first shift shows up."

"I've been in this business for twenty years," McFarland said, "and there's just no way thirty pickers could do the amount of work your laborers have been doing in just four hours. And why don't they use any of the field lights? My foreman says your people haven't used the lights set up for the second and third shifts."

"Our laborers have extremely good night vision. They work faster in the dark." Carver wondered if he was saying too much. Helen handed him the customer file. He flipped through it and pulled out a copy of the contract.

"What kind of illegal aliens do the work of two men...in the dark?"

Carver cleared his throat. "Mister McFarland, it says here in your contract that you hired us to supply no less than thirty laborers to work in your field on third shift. We're doing that, I believe. It further states that you'll keep your people away from the designated field for the entire third shift. It also says that you'll not ask the kind of questions you're asking."

"How the hell do I know what the contract says. It's not even in English."

"Yes, I know. It's a form of ancient Hebrew. The owner of TM insists on it. Some sort of tradition." Carver sighed. "I'll make sure you receive an English translation, but I have no doubt that your Sales Rep went over all these points."

"Yeah, he did. It made as much sense then as it does now. Look, if I don't get some straight answers, I'm going to have to cancel our contract."

"Oh, I don't think you'll do that, Mister McFarland. It says here that our service is creating substantial savings for you."

McFarland was silent for a moment. "Yes, it is. I'd just like some peace of mind, Carver. I want to know who's working in my field and when they'll arrive. We're going to stay on this phone until you tell me."

Carver sipped his scotch and took a deep breath. *What the hell?* McFarland didn't seem to be a bad sort. A little insistent, but nothing Carver couldn't handle. Telling him the truth shouldn't matter; it was just business. As long as McFarland was still cutting his cost by using TM, he'd remain a client. They all did.

"Mister McFarland, I'll try to shed some light on this for you. What do you know about graveyards?"

"What?"

"To be specific, the history of human interment and cemeteries."

"Not a lot, but what does—?"

"Bear with me. Thousands of years before cemeteries, when people died, they were taken to a place where their bodies, and more importantly their life essence, could be reclaimed by nature. Animals did the job, mostly. What was left, the elements took care of."

"This is fascinating stuff, but—"

"When the first cemeteries started popping up in human societies, oh...about three thousand B.C., they didn't cause a problem. The bodies and life essence could still be reclaimed by nature through the ground. The Circle of Life was not interrupted until we started using coffins. You understand about the Circle of Life?"

"Yesss..." McFarland said. "I did see *The Lion King.*"

"Well. Good." Carver cleared his throat again. "Anyway, the human life force was trapped inside the coffins, and nature wasn't able to recycle it. So nature, as nature always does, solved the problem."

"And how did it do that?"

"Over the next few centuries, a new species evolved. One that lived underground and whose sole purpose was to free the decomposing bodies from their prisons."

"Nature created the gopher to solve that problem."

Carver rolled his eyes heavenward. "No, Mister McFarland. Nature created something else, something very few humans ever get to see. A creature biologically wired to devour dead flesh, and only dead flesh. They have many names, but there is one word you may be familiar with. Have you ever heard of ghouls, Mister McFarland?"

"Oh, for crying out loud! I've just about had it with this crap. Who's your supervisor?"

"Ghouls are real, Mister McFarland. They're a relatively young species evolved for a specific purpose, but they are very real."

"So what are you saying? That you have ghouls working in my fields?'

"Since cremation became more popular, there's been a slow decline of the cemetery business. Many ghouls have been displaced and need to find new ways to live. TM Labor has been proudly employing displaced ghouls for nearly half a century."

"Jeez! That story has so much bullshit I could use it as fertilizer. So what do these ghouls look like?"

Carver shuddered. "Ghoul Relations isn't my department, but from the pictures I've seen, trust me, you don't want to know."

McFarland snorted. "So, when are your imaginary ghouls going to arrive? It's two minutes past midnight, and I haven't heard or seen a single truck."

"There won't be any trucks. They move underground, and they're very prompt. I'm sure they're in your field right now, doing their job as promised."

"Well, I don't see anybody."

"I don't know how far you live from the field, but I'm sure the vantage point from your bedroom isn't good enough to see anything, especially in the dark."

"What vantage point? I'm here in the field where your laborers are supposed to be, and I'm all alone."

Carver almost froze. "Oh, Jesus! Tell me you're joking."

"After I saw no activity out here, I got dressed, grabbed
my cell phone, and went to investigate."

Carver looked at the clock on the wall. It was three minutes
past midnight. "Christ, McFarland, get out of there!"

"What's the big deal?" McFarland sounded amused. "So I
get to glimpse your spooky workforce."

"Look, McFarland," Carver was beginning to panic. "I'll
cancel your contract; I'll refund your money, anything you want.
Just please get out of that field!"

"All right, all right, I'm walking out. What's all the urgency?"

"It's part of the deal we made with them," Carver replied,
getting his breathing under control.

"What's part of the deal?"

"That they can have anything they find: snakes, squirrels,
insects, whatever."

"Have?" McFarland asked.

"I mean kill and eat!" Carver said.

"If you're trying to scare me, it's not working."

"I don't care if you're scared. For God's sake, get out of that
field!"

"I'm going; I'm about a hundred yards from the edge. But I
have to tell you, Mister Carver, I am not happy with the way
you've spoken to me, and I'm definitely—" McFarland broke off.

"McFarland!"

Silence.

"McFarland!" Carver stood up as Helen came back into his
office. She gazed at Carver, and he could see his panic reflected
in her eyes. "McFarland, are you there?"

With a definite tremble in his voice, McFarland finally spoke.
"Carver, for the love of God."

"Have they seen you?" Carver already knew the answer.

"Oh, God. Get me out of here, Carver."

Carver's mouth went dry. "I... I can't. There is nothing..."

"They're all around me." McFarland's voice was just a whimper. "Their eyes. What's wrong with their eyes?"

Carver worked his mouth to wet his tongue. "Godspeed, Mister McFarland," he said as he held the phone away from his ear.

Helen moved forward and depressed the speaker button. Instantly, the office was alive with the sounds of struggle, a voice that tried to scream but then became choked, and then started to gag. Then, with a horrific suddenness, a sharp, grotesque crack echoed in Carver's office, sounding like a tree limb being ripped from its place on the trunk. A faded gurgling noise bled through the line as Carver returned the receiver and disengaged the speaker.

He sunk into the chair and ran his fingers through his hair. This particular tribe of ghouls didn't have any aversions to making things dead. Carver figured that the up side of being eaten by ghouls, if there was one, was that at least McFarland wouldn't be eaten alive. "We're going to need a cleanup crew in Napa, " Carver said.

"I'm on it," Helen replied. "And I'll get some client termination forms."

"Thanks, Helen." Carver held up his empty glass. "And another drink, please."

Helen glanced back on her way out. "I'll bring you the bottle." Then she closed Carver's door.

Home Care

"No!" Alice screamed.

Frantic, she bolted from the seaside cottage, nearly tearing the driftwood-colored screen door from its hinges. Alice couldn't comprehend how her father had managed to wander so far in such a brief time. She had only left the elderly man alone for a minute.

Her father, a man in the final stages of dementia, stumbled along the cliffs at the end of their property, teetering on the edge of death.

Sprinting along the dirt path leading toward the cliffs, Alice continued calling to him. She knew that, even if he had heard her panicked cries, it was unlikely he would respond. His terminal condition had robbed her father of a mind that had earned two doctorates. What remained was an intermittent consciousness that moved in and out like bad TV reception.

When Alice realized how bad he was, she started the fight to bring him home, to release him from a rundown state facility, and struggled even harder to get awarded the right to manage the end of his life.

He wasn't going to perish in the care of nameless strangers who had no idea who he was. And he wasn't going to die in some stupid accident, not after Alice had navigated the bureaucracy, the courts, and scrapped together everything she had to pay the attorney's fees. He was finally home and in her charge. But an instant of diverted attention allowed him to slip the veil of supervision, move off the back porch, and stagger straight for the cliffs. It was all about to end in a meaningless accident.

"No," Alice screamed. *Not like this.*

The elderly man's foot wobbled, loose gravel rolling like marbles unsteadied each step. Alice's heart leaped into her throat watching her father begin to sway.

She sprinted faster than she thought possible, closing the gap quickly. She sent thoughts forward like lifelines, trying to will her father steady. *No, please. Just hold on.*

She tried not to picture his broken body at the bottom, strewn across jagged rocks, the sea threatening at his shattered limbs. *Please let me make it.* She had to make it. She *needed* to make it.

Alice pushed the image of an unexpected end from her mind and reached out, stretching every muscle. As her father started to fall over the edge, Alice's fingers dug into his sweater like a rake churning the soil.

She wrenched back, easily righting the frail man. Spinning him around, his eyes went wide. For a moment, he seemed confused. Then slowly, with growing awareness, recognition sparked on his face. It was a rare thing, a momentary gift, and Alice smiled as a tear traced the outline of her nose.

"Alice," he said. "What're you doing here?"

A faint chuckle escaped her lips. "What am I doing here?" she asked through heavy breaths, shaking her head. She gazed into her father's glassy eyes, feeling her relief at saving him suddenly melt away. The icy resolve that drove most of what she did froze her features as childhood memories rushed into her mind's eye. She could see by the ghost-white dread blanketing his face that those same memories were coming back to him— memories of his little girl and what he'd done with that little girl.

Alice looked into his eyes, something she felt an unflinching need to do. They were not the eyes of a frail man near death, unable to remember his daughter's name, but of a monster, a demon that prayed on its own.

From a place of unending pain, where dark memories cast a shadow on all she had become, Alice summoned the strength to put both hands flat on his chest. She narrowed her gaze, drew in a cleansing breath, and exhaled long and hard.

Then she pushed.

The Day Hypnotism
Died

Hypnotists.

I didn't believe in them. Most people don't. We chalk it up to mentalist bunk, sleight of hand for the unconscious, only effective on the weak- or feeble-minded. But disbelief can dissolve in the span of a moment when evidence to the contrary rips your friends away in a cacophony of blood and screaming.

This is about just such a moment, one in which I met the greatest living hypnotist in the world. It was also the moment I lost three good friends for reasons I still don't understand. I'm not sure anyone does.

"So, Runt. What's this great idea you have?" I had asked as the evening began, the four of us strolling toward the boardwalk. We were four nerdy, dateless high school seniors looking for action, or as close as we could get to it.

"Stop calling me that," James, the smallest of us, said, pushing up his glasses.

Russell slapped a beefy hand on my back, and I felt his enormous girth in the friendly thump. "Yeah, Craig. Stop calling Runt that." He chuckled, always laughing at his own comments, thinking himself the next Chris Farley.

James stopped and turned around, glaring. "I hate it when Coach Hanson calls me that, and I sure as hell don't like it when my friends do it."

James had been called Runt since before I met him, so it was always a little surprising when he got pissed about it. "Sorry," I said, gesturing to myself, shrugging. "I'm an ass."

James continued glaring, his face turning pink.

"Sorry," I repeated. "Really." Sighing, I took a step toward him, holding my arms wide. "Hug?"

A smile moved over James's face. "Go blow an Orc."

I heard Russell and Allen laugh as I dropped my arms.

Allen, taller than all of us, stepped forward. "Okay, now that you girls have made up..." He looked at James. "What's this great idea?"

James reached into his back pocket, producing a flyer. It looked old, like some pirate's treasure map, with charred edges and faded black ink. It was all for show, but it was intriguing. He held it out so we could all read it.

One Night Only!
The Greatest Hypnotist in the World!
South End of the Fun-Zone

"The Fun-Zone?" I said.

James met my eyes. "Forgot, you're a newbie."

"It's this carnival that comes to the boardwalk every spring break," Russell said.

I nodded. "Any good?"

"No," James said. "Mostly kid crap. But this hypnotist thing sounds like just the place for hip guys like us to make an appearance."

I smiled. "If we were hip, we'd have dates."

"Dates?" Allen said. "We're keeping our options open."

"Yeah, that's it." I nodded. "Okay, Runt... Uh, James. Lead on."

We strolled through the Fun-Zone, stopping only to lose some coin at the carnival games, none of us coming close to winning anything. At the south end, we saw a modest circus tent set far enough apart to make me think it wasn't associated with the carnival.

"Jeez, look at the line," Allen said.

"Hey, does that say admission fifteen bucks?" Russell pointed a thick finger ahead.

"Wow, that's steep," I said.

James faced us. "Come on, ya tightwads. What else do you have to spend it on? Girlfriends?"

"Better be a good show," Russell said as we stepped in line.

By the time we made it inside, there were no seats left. People stood along the tent walls, looking impatient.

At the side of the stage, I saw a slender redheaded woman wearing a shimmering spandex outfit and carrying more folding chairs than she could handle. I didn't hesitate. "Follow me."

My friends fell in line, and we were in a good position when she began unfolding the chairs on the left side of the stage. Russell helped her place the last few, and then we took our seats. She smiled at him, saying, "Danke."

Russell leaned over. "What'd she say?"

My high school German had finally come in handy. "She said, Thank you."

"You think German women like big guys?" Russell patted his belly.

I was about to say not a chance in hell when the lights suddenly dimmed.

A yellowish spotlight flickered to life, dowsing the stage in a sickly hue. Stepping into the light—from where I couldn't tell—

was a tall man dressed in a white tuxedo. His face was unremarkable. The kind you would forget only moments after looking away. Even today, I can't recall a single identifying feature. The only thing that lingers with me is that he seemed wrong for the moment. I got the sense that he shouldn't really be there. Not with us anyway. Like an Ann Rice character, he seemed like someone merely passing through this century.

Without a word or facial expression, the man began to conduct a symphony of magic tricks. Boring stuff—a rabbit out of a hat, interlocking rings, and a lousy sleight-of-hand card trick. Even the music was cheesy. It sounded like there was an organ grinder backstage, turning the crank without any sense of rhythm. I half expected a monkey in a fez and matching vest to start working the crowd for pocket change.

After each trick, there was some polite applause, but most just groaned.

"If this shit keeps up, I'm going to kill Runt," Russell whispered in my ear.

"Right after we get our money back," I said.

Suddenly the hypnotist bowed, still not saying a word, and the stage went dark. There was a smattering of uneasy applause, the kind you might expect after a really bad karaoke performance.

In the dim light, we all glared a James. Our undersized friend seemed to shrivel under our collective, disapproving gaze.

The spotlight returned with a suddenness that made me gasp. This time it was deep crimson, and the redhead from before stepped onto the stage. She brought her hands up to her mid-section, interlocking them like a ballerina, and began to speak. Her words seemed purposely slow, seemingly aware that her accent was cumbersome to understand. "You may have heard that hypnotism is the power of suggestion, allowing subjects to believe what others cannot perceive. Many lay claim to these powers. Sideshow frauds, praying on willing minds, degrading the art, and offending the Masters."

She paused long enough for a few murmurs to bubble up from the audience and then continued. "What you will see tonight is real hypnotism, not the usual carnival freak show you have all come to expect. On this stage, the wall separating perception and reality will become transparent, and you will see as the hypnotist sees. Fantasy and belief will become one, and as a final act, before becoming a part of the ages, my Master will remove the wall between what was once thought and what can only be imagined. This evening is the final performance of the last living Master, and it should be remembered as the night hypnotism died."

"What the hell," Russell whispered.

"That was a bit dramatic," I said.

The lights came up over the audience, and the woman looked out onto the crowd, her expression suddenly pleasant, as if she was a hostess at a dinner party and had just noticed her guests. "Now, for those of you that wish to become a part of a performance that will be talked about for a century, please join me," she said, gesturing to the stage.

A thin brunette woman stood up in the front row, and the redhead waved her up. Several others stood, moving toward the stage. Then to my amazement, James stood up. He must have thought that whatever was going to happen to him on stage was less severe than what we were thinking about doing to him for dragging us in here.

Then Russell stood up, his wide hips bumping my shoulder.

"What are you doing?" I said.

Russell shrugged. "Just thought I'd get a closer look at the hypnotist's assistant."

Our two friends walked up on stage as Allen and I stared at each other across two empty chairs. He tilted his head. "You chicken?"

I narrowed my eyes. "I will if you will." I rocked forward,

looking as if I was about to stand up.

Allen jumped to his feet.

Sucker.

I sat back in my chair, arms folded.

He glared at me, shoulders slumped. "You suck."

The redhead waved at Allen to join the others on stage. He shot me one last disapproving leer as he walked toward the spotlight.

I looked up at my three friends, very pleased with myself. They stood side by side with five other volunteers, all looking anxious, excited. Russell motioned at me to join them on stage. I just shook my head, grinning. Allen cupped his hands around his lips and mouthed the word, *Wussy.* At least, I think that's what he said.

I mouthed in returned, *Bite me.*

The hypnotist appeared on stage, and again I didn't notice from where. For whatever reason, his assistant did most of the talking. She asked the volunteers to focus on the hypnotist's index finger, which he raised and held out at arm's length. Without a word, he lowered and lifted it over and over. He did this for a full minute, and I could feel the crowd growing restless. The thin brunette even started to giggle, but the redheaded assistant gave her a harsh glare, and she immediately stopped.

After another grueling minute of this, the hypnotist lowered his hand, and as his hand descended, so did the eyelids of the volunteers. All of them. By the time the man's hand was at his side, my friends' heads were all slumped onto one shoulder.

My jaw dropped.

There were chortles from the crowd. Not the type spawned from a humorous situation, but the kind emitted from a large group of people who are collectively unsure how to react.

The redhead looked out over the crowd, holding a finger to her smiling lips. "They sleep now." Her voice was an intense whisper.

No shit. I shifted in my seat—excitement, concern, fear, and anticipation coursing through my body. I was already imagining telling this story to everyone, even though the people I would most likely tell were up on stage.

The hypnotist turned to face the crowd and made a brief gesture, like a man tipping his hat to an elegant lady he chances upon on the street. Then, with the commanding presence of a conductor, he turned to face his subjects, instruments ready to be played.

He snapped his fingers, and the volunteers awoke, their eyelids fluttering like window shades. Laughter rose from the crowd as the volunteers yawned; some even stretched as if waking from a long sleep.

Allen looked at me, yawning. He shrugged his shoulders as if to say, *What happened?* I just returned his unspoken query with a grin, nodding.

The crowd quieted, and my attention again fell upon the hypnotist. With poised strides, he moved over to the right of the stage, standing in front of a volunteer furthest in line from my friends.

The volunteer, a man in his mid-forties, smiled as the hypnotist gazed into his eyes. I could tell the man was uncomfortable with this. He seemed to arc backward, like a weed bending in a strong wind.

The hypnotist moved in, their noses coming close to touching. He stayed there for a moment, a voyeur peeking into a window. The volunteer gazed back, his eyes never blinking.

The crowd fell silent, and when the hypnotist finally pulled back to speak a single word, it resonated to all four corners of the tent. Without any hint of an accent, he said, "Spider."

The volunteer's eyes slammed shut, and he dropped onto the center of the stage with a *thud*. His round belly lay flat as his arms and legs began to spread outward, grasping for something. Then his hands gripped the stage, and he pushed himself up, rising slowly, like a predator searching through the grass for its next meal. His head sunk into his shoulders, and his neck just seemed to have retracted inside his body.

It was horribly uncomfortable to look at, and the crowd gasped, myself included. I could hear people behind me murmur to one another. "Jeez, that's incredible."

"How did he... Knees don't bend that way."

"It's just a show. The volunteers are all plants."

The redhead raised her hands in an attempt to quiet the crowd. The rumblings lessened a bit, but continued. Then the man on all fours started to rotate, and the crowd fell still. Soon his rear end pointed at the audience, and after a brief hesitation, he started to crawl. A shiver scaled my spine as I watched him scurry across the stage, not with the motion of a being using four legs but with the dexterity of a creature with eight. The four limbs I could see moved in tandem with four unseen limbs, and although they remained invisible, I had no doubt they were there.

The back of the stage, shrouded in shadow, appeared to be the man's destination, and my throat went dry as he crawled to the safety of the dark. He spun around, sinking into the blackness, with just his head visibly bobbing up and down about a foot off the stage; his pupils, now black, glinted in the stage lights.

I could feel his humanity slipping away as he looked back at the crowd, no longer recognizing us, and the audience no longer seeing a man.

Stunned applause rose from the crowd, but the hypnotist did not stop to acknowledge this. He stepped over, standing in front of the next volunteer, a thin brunette woman. After a similar preamble, the hypnotist said, "Chicken."

The woman's eyes fell shut, and she hunched slightly. When they opened, her head started darting forward, her arms curled up on her sides, flapping.

The hypnotist removed a handful of chicken feed from his pocket, holding it out in front of her. The woman's head darted forward, pecking at the pile in his hand.

The crowd again broke out into reserved applause.

The hypnotist let the feed fall to the floor, and he slapped his hands together. The woman fell to her knees, pecking at the food on the stage as the hypnotist took a moment to glance back at the crowd. Although there was no expression on his face, I got the distinct impression that he despised us. Maybe it was in his eyes, but in that moment, I felt absolute loathing.

He turned to the next volunteer as his assistant brought out a large wicker basket. The assistant gestured for the volunteer to step into it, which he did, smiling as if it were something he did every day. The hypnotist peered into the man's eyes and said, "King Cobra."

The volunteer dropped into the basket, disappearing from view. A moment later, he began to rise, not as a man would stand up, but like a serpent ascending to the tune of a snake charmer. The hypnotist took a noticeable fast step back, as if he wanted to stay out of striking range.

There was some applause that lacked enthusiasm and grew more uneasy. My own hands lay in my lap, unable to move.

The hypnotist gave a nod to his assistant. She stepped behind the basket, its lid in her hand, and raised it over the volunteer's head. In one quick motion, she pushed the lid down, forcing the volunteer back into the basket. She wedged it in tight, then glanced at the hypnotist, who had already moved on.

The next volunteer became a weasel, who immediately arched his body into an unsavory position and began grooming a very long tail, seen only by him. The hypnotist next did his thing with a petite woman, who, believing herself a gazelle, leaped off the stage, bounded down the central aisle and out the entrance. A man in the crowd, a husband or boyfriend, jumped to his feet and ran after her, calling, "Linda?"

I looked up at my friends, who all waited patiently, like they were standing in line at a public restroom. I waved at them to get their attention. They looked down at me, perplexed, seemingly unaware of the other volunteers' metamorphosis. I motioned for them to get off the stage, and before I knew it, I was on my feet, heart pounding, my gestures growing frantic.

Popcorn hit me in the back, and I heard someone say, "Sit down." Another volley of popcorn and something sticky hit my head, so I slowly lowered myself back into my seat.

The hypnotist stood in front of Allen, looking him up and down. He gazed into my friend's eyes and said, "Monkey." Allen dropped into a squat, his legs tucking under his body, shrinking. He rocked forward on his knuckles, and his tongue shot out over his lips.

The hypnotist patted him on the head, then pointed to a thick wood post that held up the tent's roof. Allen furrowed a simian brow, then jumped off the stage, his butt inches above the ground. When he reached the post, he leaped up, his sandals falling from his feet.

I held my breath as I watched him climb the pole like someone born to it. When he neared the ceiling, he stopped and looked down. The hypnotist produced a banana from his pocket and threw it up.

Allen, I swear, caught it with his foot. His goddamn foot.

I could hear the audience applauding, but it was like distant background noise—the soundtrack to a movie I wish I wasn't watching.

The hypnotist turned to Russell. My friend's huge frame towered over the hypnotist, but it cast no illusion about who was in control. The hypnotist leaned forward and said, "Mouse."

Russell dropped to the floor. I could feel the *thud* reverberate under my chair. His nearly three-hundred-pound body seemed to shrivel, limbs retracting, fingers curling into paws. He looked at me with no recognition, nose twitching with unseen whiskers. Russell's beady eyes scanned the crowd, and it looked as if he were about to run. But just then, the assistant placed a large, clear plastic bowl, face down, on top of Russell's head. Russell froze.

Laughter began to filter through the audience as we realized Russell believed himself to be trapped inside the bowl. Russell sniffed at the wall of his prison as the crowd clapped.

The hypnotist stepped in front of James, gazing deep. James cocked his head a little, as if he might be in pain, but then he straightened.

"I know what a runt like you wants to be," the hypnotist said. It was the only sentence I heard him say. He took several steps back, giving James a large berth, then he said, "Elephant."

James's head slumped forward, as if the weight of a trunk pulled it down, and he landed on all fours. The stage shook, and I could hear wood cracking. He thrashed his head from side to side, and I felt a breeze, almost as if a large set of ears were moving the air like enormous fans. James raised his head and bellowed so loud I covered my ears.

The crowd went silent.

Near James's feet, the woman believing herself a chicken pecked at the seeds on the stage. James stepped back, looking irritated, and brought his head up high again. I thought he was going to make that awful, inhuman sound again, but in the soft tent light filtering through the dust that wafted up from the stage, I saw an outline extending from James's face. Like an apparition, it hung there, thick, long, and ghostly. Although I recognized what it was, I still didn't believe it. It was a trunk. An elephant's trunk.

James swung it downward in a horrific arch, putting his whole head and upper body into the motion. It caught the woman pecking at the stage across the mid-section, lifted her up, and hurled her into the air. She crashed into the back curtain, causing the man, now a spider, to scurry out of the darkness.

I could hear screams behind me as I looked at the broken woman lying at the back of the stage. She wasn't moving.

My eye caught the hypnotist as he stepped over to Russell, still trapped inside a bowl. People were knocking into me and toppling chairs, and I struggled to stay where I was. The hypnotist placed a hand on the bowl on Russell's head and drummed his fingers. He looked out onto the pandemonium, and I saw it again—that look of contempt in his eyes.

He lifted the bowl with a quick movement, and Russell wasted no time. He darted forward, nose twitching, beady eyes scanning back and forth. Then he seemed to catch sight of the man who believed himself a weasel, and he froze. The weasel met the rodent's gaze and began to pounce. Russell retreated toward James, the weasel in fast pursuit. The two began running around James in wide circles. James was getting upset and started rising on his hind legs and stomping his front feet down, shaking the stage.

I rushed forward, reaching out, intending to grab Russell, but the mouse had scurried under one of James' front feet just as it came down. The next thing I heard was a grotesque popping, like a watermelon in a trash compactor.

The crushing sound was still echoing in my ear when James raised his foot, which had just reduced the midsection of Russell's enormous girth to the width of a pizza box.

James continued to stomp, transforming Russell's head into a pulpy mass of gelatin. The stage began to sway, and I could hear wood splintering, metal tearing from where it was screwed into the wood. Someone careened into my chest, spinning me toward the tent's entrance, the only exit, now clogged with bodies. Over the screaming, I could hear the canvas rending as new exits were created along the tent walls.

Even though there seemed no point, James still brought his foot down on Russell's remains over and over again. Unable to endure the pounding, the stage collapsed with a crash so loud it momentarily drowned out the sounds of panic. The large wicker basket toppled into the seats, its lid rolling down the aisle. The man inside began to slither out.

The collapsing of the stage had somehow calmed James, and I started moving toward him. I didn't know if I could snap him out of this, but I sure as hell was going to try. I approached him from the side, just behind his peripheral vision. I was about to stretch out my hands, preparing to clasp his shoulders when I hit something.

My face collided with a leathery but soft surface. I put my hands up, feeling the thick, wrinkled skin. I blinked my eyes but could not see what my hands had touched.

As my fingers slid over thick folds of warm flesh, I felt tiny sporadic hairs bending beneath my palms, and as I brushed over them, their pale outlines began to flicker into view. I stared at my hands caressing the air, watching them rise up and down slightly. Looking through my fingers at James, I realized that my hands rose up and down as James breathed.

My friend looked back at me, his head craning around as if it swiveled on a large neck. Indifference glinted in his eyes. He turned forward and started lumbering toward the center aisle.

Something caught me hard on the side, and I toppled back. Reflecting, I can only imagine what struck me was James's unseen rear leg or hip as his elephant exterior moved past me.

I landed on the front row of chairs, my head cracking against a seat. Blood trickled into my eye as I pushed myself up. My first thought was to look for James, but something overhead caught my attention. High up on the tent ceiling, a man defied gravity and moved like an arachnid, clinging to the canvas. His sunken black eyes gazed down, and I swear to God, it looked as if he were trying to spin a web.

A banana peel landed on my head, and I heard Allen, still

high above the seats, laugh like a chimpanzee. I slapped the peel from my scalp and looked down the aisle.

Wooden chairs had been reduced to splinters under James's weight. I had just caught sight of him as he moved out the exit, his unseen bulk catching in the opening's aluminum frame. The metal twisted, and the entire tent shifted in the direction James was walking. I thought it would come down around me, but then he broke free, and the whole canvas room snapped back with a violent jolt.

I hustled down the aisle, jumping over the wreckage. When I reached the exit, I looked back at the collapsed stage. I think I wanted to get one last look at the hypnotist, the being responsible for all this chaos, try to remember his face, mark it in my mind so I could identify him later. But he and his assistant were gone.

The only thing I saw was a man, now free from his basket, coiling himself around the broken, still body of the woman James had hurled through the air. Running out of the tent, I tried to force from my mind the image of the man attempting to swallow the dead woman whole.

James's trail wasn't hard to pick up. I just followed the crushed cars, injured people, and the screams. By the time I had caught up to him, a county deputy was trying to block his path. The officer stood in the middle of the street, directly in front of James. People who had seen the destruction were yelling at him to move, but the young deputy stood his ground.

"Get out of the way," I screamed, running just behind James. I waved my arms to the side. "Just move."

The officer must have thought he was dealing with a drunk, but he must have seen something at the last second because he went for his gun. The muzzle had just cleared the holster when James hit him.

The deputy hit the ground hard, and I cringed at the familiar popping sound. He managed a scream that was instantly silenced as a large foot crushed the man's head.

I tried not to look as I stepped by, but my peripheral vision caught one of the man's legs, still twitching, glistening crimson in the downward glow of a streetlamp.

I followed my friend, watching him career into parked cars like the town drunk. He seemed disorientated, frightened, but he never stopped moving. I tried talking to him, but there just wasn't enough humanity left in there to hear me.

Despite his lack of response, I tried for the next ten blocks to reach him, calling his name, pleading with him to stop as the sounds of emergency vehicles moved around us. Nearing the edge of town, we both turned a corner, and I saw a barricade of black-and-whites blocking our path. I could tell by the number of weapons drawn that the cops were not interested in apprehending James. I'm guessing that ship had sailed when James crushed a deputy under four tons of unseen elephant flesh.

I dropped to the ground, hoping James would do the same, but when he noticed the police line, he slowed for a few steps, then charged. I felt bullets cut through the air before I heard them. I covered my head. When I finally looked up, James was on his knees, shots still tearing into him.

I don't know what the police could see. Did they see an unarmed, overweight, seventeen-year-old kid, or did they see something else? I like to think they saw something that terrified them, something to justify emptying their weapons. The shooting didn't stop until a burly voice yelled, "Cease fire."

I envisioned myself running over to James, holding him in my arms to hear his final words as they do in the movies, but when I started to get up, the same gruff voice yelled, "Don't move, asshole. Put your hands out where we can see them."

Twenty minutes later, I was still wearing the handcuffs the owner of that burly voice—Sheriff Kinkade—had slapped on my wrists. He questioned me in the back of the squad car, his large

Stetson rubbing against the roof.

"How well did you know the deceased?" Kinkade asked.

"He was my friend," I said. "We called him Runt."

That was just over a year ago. I spent some time trying to track down the hypnotist, as did Sheriff Kinkade and a few private detectives hired by relatives of the nine confirmed victims from that night. At least three others are still missing. From their pictures in the paper, I recognized them as other volunteers, and after all this time, I'm pretty sure their families, at least if they knew what I knew, would prefer that they stay missing.

One of the volunteers who isn't missing is my friend Allen, and I'm ashamed to admit it, but I can't bring myself to visit him anymore. He's been a resident of the Riverdale County Mental Institute since that night. I stopped driving up to see him shortly after hair started to sprout all over his body. Sheriff Kinkade said he looks like something that stepped out of *Planet of the Apes*. Allen shares a floor at the sanitarium with a teenager who hunts rodents with the cunning of a weasel and a woman who leaps around like a gazelle.

I don't think the hypnotist's final performance will ever fade into the past for me. My nightmares keep it in the forefront of my mind, and every animal I see in the wake of day always has some human feature that makes me wonder. Today I received a news clipping in the mail from Sheriff Kinkade. It described how he and his men were called when someone found a monster-sized cobra. It had been nesting under the boardwalk, feeding on cats, dogs, and—some think—the children who have gone missing. How a cobra had managed to make it to the United States was still a mystery, but what was more concerning were the strange appendages that ran along its underbelly. According to eye-witness reports, they resembled human fingers.

Pumpkin Seeds

Halloween jack-o'-lanterns decorated the Linden's front porch. Their soft glow illuminated Mark Linden's dazed expression. Sheriff Kinkade tried to appear positive as he put a gentle hand on Mark's shoulder. Having no family of his own, Kinkade could only imagine what Mark was going through.

"Is there anyone we can call?" Kinkade hunkered down a bit so his thick six-foot frame didn't tower over Mark as much.

Mark's eyes were shut, and Kinkade waited patiently for him to speak. He knew Mark was an educated man, the kind who kept up with current events. Mark would know that his wife wasn't dead. Not yet.

The *Daily Gazette* article had been very detailed, more so than Kinkade liked, about the M.O. of the Riverdale Snatcher.

Mark's eyes opened. "How long do we have...'til she's found?"

The time between abduction and the discovery of the bodies, ritualistically pinned up like a frog on a dissection slab, varied, from two to five days. Away from the press, the FBI had shared with Kinkade that it depended on how much gratification the Snatcher was deriving from the current victim.

"We're gonna find her," Kinkade said. "Long before..."

"I just took the kids out trick-or-treating. We were only gone a half-hour. I can't believe—oh, God, Carrie." Mark sobbed into both hands.

"We'll find her." Kinkade tried to remember what church the Lindens attended. It wasn't St. Andrews because that's where he went. "Do you go to First Community?"

Mark nodded, his hands still covering his face.

"Would you like me to call Pastor Johansson? I'm sure he c—" From the corner of his eye, Kinkade saw one of his deputies waving at him from the sidewalk. "Excuse me a minute, Mark."

Kinkade started down the porch steps. By the time his foot hit the grass, he was angry. Whatever reason Deputy Simon had for interrupting, Kinkade knew it would be either trivial or just plain stupid. Most of Kinkade's deputies were kids fresh out of high school, and not one of them had enough confidence to handle anything on their own. It was infuriating to a veteran like Kinkade, a man with fifteen years as a city cop and two tours of duty in the Marines.

Kinkade met the deputy in the middle of the lawn. "What the hell is so goddamn important you need to interrupt me every ten seconds, Simon?"

Looking down, Simon seemed to be searching for words in the vicinity of his shoelaces. "You know how you told me to take pictures of the crime scene?"

Kinkade was hoping to get some shots before the FBI showed up and shut him out again. "Yeah. Did you forget the camera?"

"No, Sir, I brought it," the Deputy said. "Batteries are dead, though. Been meaning to swing by the Walgreens for some new ones."

Kinkade shook his head. He recalled reviewing the man's resume, and he was pretty sure there weren't any bullet points that said, "Idiot" or "First-class Moron." *Why did I hire this guy?*

"I have a camera in my trunk, so never mind that. Here's

what I want you to do," Kinkade said.

Simon nodded, taking out a notepad.

"Take Mark inside to be with his kids. Then, call Pastor Johansson. Tell him what's happened and ask him to come over. Then call Carrie Linden's sister. Think she's in Idlewood. I'm sure Mark would want her here. Times like this, a man needs the support of the Lord and his family."

Simon stopped writing and then started reading aloud. "Uh, take Mister Linden inside, call Pastor Johansson and sister in Idlewood. Got it." The deputy slapped his notebook shut and marched off toward the house.

Kinkade felt an eye roll coming on, but he stopped it, sighed instead, then headed to the street. His squad car, parked at the curb, had a disposable camera in the glove box, but he hoped that he'd left his digital in the trunk. When he reached the rear of the car, he paused, remembering the huge mess he'd left in there. To find his camera, he was going to have to dig.

Glancing back at the porch, Kinkade wanted to make sure Simon was following instructions. The orders seemed simple enough, but that had never stopped Simon from screwing them up before. Simon escorted Mark into the house. He shut the door, leaving the porch vacant, save for three jack-o'-lanterns, eyes glowing orange.

Their devilishly carved eyes cast an almost knowing stare at Kinkade. A chill crept over his neck, and he slapped it away. He'd never liked jack-o'-lanterns. Damn things gave him the willies.

He popped the trunk and peered inside. Yep, it was a full-on mess. *Jeez, the camera is probably at the bottom.*

He reached in and lifted Carrie Linden's bound feet off the spare tire, then tried to roll her further back. She still appeared to be unconscious from the blow he'd delivered to the back of her head.

No sign of the camera.

When Kinkade grabbed a fist full of her hair to lift her head, her eyes popped open. She tried to scream through her gag— a sock shoved so far down her throat only the torn fringes of the toe section dangled outside her bleeding lips. Kinkade leaned in, putting his face inches from hers. "Don't even think about it. Make one sound and I'll pull that tongue right out of your pretty little head."

Carrie Linden blinked and sank back into the trunk.

"That's better," Kinkade said. "Besides, there will be plenty of time for screaming later." He released her hair and slammed the trunk closed.

He glanced back at the Linden's porch, prepared to meet the watchful leer of the glowing jack-o'-lanterns. But there were two more pairs of eyes staring back at him that he hadn't prepared himself for.

Mark and Deputy Simon stood on the porch, looking astonished.

Kinkade shook his head. *Simon, you're such a screw-up.* The instructions were simple. *Take Mark inside, call Johansson, call the sister. What the hell were they doing on the porch?*

The deputy went for his gun but had trouble releasing the holster strap.

Kinkade knew that hiring deputies who made Barney Fife look competent would prove beneficial at some point. He cocked his head and swiftly pulled his revolver, leveling it at the deputy. Before Simon could get his weapon free, Kinkade fired.

The deputy was hit square in the chest and fell back against the house. As he slid down the wall, he finally managed to unholster his pistol. The gun fell into his lap when his butt hit the porch.

Kinkade turned the revolver on Mark. The frightened man dove out of the way. Kinkade fired twice, trying to hit Mark in mid-leap, but his shots shattered the living room window instead. Mark landed out of sight, knocking a few uncarved pumpkins off the porch railing.

Screams came from inside the house. *The kids*, Kinkade thought. *Jeez, I'm in no mood to kill kids.*

Neighborhood dogs started barking, porch lights came on, and behind him, a screen door squeaked open across the street. *Damn.* He lowered his weapon. *Time to move on.* This town was about tapped out anyway.

Kinkade stepped around to the driver's side of his squad car and reached for the door handle. A speeding glint of orange reflected in the car window. When he turned, the pumpkin hit him in the face. The blow knocked him back against the car. His head cracked against the lights on the roof.

He slid down onto the grass, wiping pumpkin guts from his eyes. The juices stung. Pumpkin seeds slid down his cheeks like unwanted tears. His fingers grazed his nose, and he winced in pain. It was probably broken.

Kinkade should have been angry, but he wasn't. Mark was now fumbling around Simon's body.

Nice throw, big guy.

Kinkade searched for his gun in the pumpkin innards on the ground. His piece had fallen into the gutter, hammer still cocked. He picked it up as Mark came down the steps, holding something out in front of him.

Kinkade's eyes focused with a suddenness that made him blink. He brought his revolver up. Mark had Simon's gun and was rushing across the lawn, pointing the weapon while frantically searching for the safety.

Kinkade chuckled. *That's the spirit. Fight for it.* Kinkade aimed and pulled the trigger.

But nothing happened.

He pulled again. Nothing.

He examined the revolver and couldn't believe his eyes. Pumpkin seeds, wedged in like a doorstop, were keeping the hammer from falling. He pushed the seeds out with his thumb, then quickly brought the revolver up again.

A pistol shot boomed and flashed before his eyes. The first shot hit his chest like a baseball bat to the ribs. The second and third pierced his gut with the burning intensity of branding irons.

When the shooting ended, Mark stood before him, silhouetted in the porch light. He was still pointing Simon's pistol at Kinkade's chest and, shaking like a child, kept pulling the trigger. *Click, click, click.*

"Good job, Cowboy," Kinkade said, coughing up blood. He brought his hand to his face. Pumpkin juice dripped down his fingers, mixing with splatters of crimson.

Kinkade convulsed and pulled in a last shallow breath as he glanced up at the Lindens' porch. Maybe he was hallucinating, but he swore that the jack-o'-lanterns were grinning at him. Twisted grins with glowing malevolence.

Then, just before he died, Kinkade remembered... He didn't actually see Mark throw the pumpkin.

Piercing the Dead

I'm a lot of things: adulterer, barroom brawler, and—if you count the war—killer. But I'm no liar. So it rubbed me wrong to have to fib to my granddaughter when she asked me who the strangest person to ever come into my shop was. Telling her the truth would have been a sin. No twelve-year-old needs to know that the things going bump in the night aren't always products of imagination. She doesn't need to know that monsters are real.

Hell, I'm in my fifties, and I wish I didn't know. But there is no going back—not after that night.

It started out just like any other night. The sun fell out of the sky fast, plunging Austin's Sixth Street Club District into darkness—the kind of darkness that seemed to be an open invitation for the city's night things. Neo-punkers, hipsters, and bar-hoppers spilled out into the street. All believed the night was theirs. All believed they would live forever.

I own the Ink Spot Tattoo and Piercing Parlor on the south end of Sixth Street. There's a head shop on my left and a New Age bookstore to the right, where all the young Wiccan gals seemed to gather. I'd see them as they walked by my window—their long hair resting on flowing cloaks. Makes me wish I were twenty again.

On this particular August evening, I had just walked into the shop after my nightly viewing of the Mexican free-tailed bats leaving the Congress Avenue Bridge. I had seen it a thousand times. Watching a black cloud comprised of over a million bats leaving all at once in search of food never ceased to fill me with wonder.

My assistant Chloe greeted me. "How were the bats?"

"Hungry." It was my standard reply.

She checked out early that night, leaving me alone to pierce and tattoo the dozen or so college kids who would eventually stagger in.

By a little past eleven, three girls sat in the waiting room and one in my chair. I was doing a quick touch-up on a heart-shaped rose that had faded from too much exposure to spring break when out of the corner of my eye I saw a very tall black woman speaking with the girls in the waiting area. Didn't notice her come in, but the hum of the needle draws most of my focus.

When I had a second to look up, she was handing out money. Each girl quickly snatched some cash from the stranger and promptly left my establishment. Then the woman had the gall to turn my open sign to closed.

By this point, my blood pressure was rising, so I stopped work and set the needle on my knee. An angry hand never does good work. The woman strolled to the back of the store, as if her actions were the most natural thing in the world. Without addressing me, she looked down at the girl in my chair. "Sweetie, how about you come back some other evenin', and it'll be on me."

The girl in the chair looked at the two hundred-dollar bills held out to her, then back at me.

With a sigh, I held up my hands in surrender, and the girl

jumped out of my chair.

In the span of a minute, my establishment had emptied, and I was alone with this tall, gaunt woman. Her hair was cut so close to her scalp that I swear it was painted on. She wore a leather mini-skirt, black patent leather boots, and a tight-fitting blouse with a diverse array of zippers. A long scarf completely concealed her slender neck. She looked Caribbean or Creole—probably from New Orleans or thereabouts.

Still pretty pissed, I gazed into her brown eyes. "You just sent about a thousand dollars' worth of business out the door, honey." It was closer to three or four hundred, but I'm prone to exaggeration, especially when aggravated. "Can you give me one good reason why I don't bounce your butt outta here?"

She reached into her coffin-shaped purse and pulled out some money. I had never seen a thousand-dollar bill, let alone two.

"I need a piercing done. I heard you were good," she said.

In the greedy glare of all those zeros, my anger evaporated. I snatched the bills and tucked them into my shirt pocket.

"First things first, though. The security cameras, they feed into a VCR?" She pointed to the three cameras mounted around the shop.

"Yeah. Won't be much help to the cops catchin' the guy who blows my brains out if they weren't." I pointed to the VCR strapped under my worktable.

She stepped forward, bent over, then popped the tape out. "If you don't mind?" Fact was, I did mind, but there was two thousand dollars in my pocket that seemed to scream, *No, ya don't, dummy!*

"What kind of piercing do you have in mind?"

"Not me." She grinned, showing teeth. "Him." She gestured to the front of the shop.

My first thought upon seeing the figure in my waiting room was, *Okay, there's a dead man in my shop.* But then it started shuffling toward me. *Now, I've got a walking dead man in my shop.*

As the man approached, it became painfully clear that he was deathly ill. His complexion was bloodless, and sweat dripped from his features. It was a hot August night, but not that hot, not by a long shot. When he was a few feet away, his body went into some kind of convulsion, flailing against the wall.

Creole Lady rushed forward, draped his arm over her shoulder, then dragged him to the chair. Strong gal. Stronger than she looked.

"What's the matter with him?" I said.

"Doesn't travel well. He'll be fine."

His face was that of a corpse. I could see dark veins beneath his translucent skin as if the blood in them had stopped flowing a while ago. I wanted to say, *This boy needs a mortician, not a piercing,* but I settled for, "I think he needs a doctor."

"They can't help him," she said. "Now, let's get this done." I looked into the man's eyes. They were hauntingly gray and very old. Ancient.

I realized at that point that I wanted Creole Lady and Zombie Man out of my shop as fast as I could get them gone. "All right, I have a selection of stainless steel posts, studs, and hoops over here. What did—"

"No, I have one." From her purse, she pulled a small leather box. Embroidered on the top was an ankh. It wasn't an uncommon symbol, especially after that movie with David Bowie that I never got around to seeing. Supposed to be Egyptian or something—means everlasting life.

She pulled the lid back, revealing a chrome post of a very thick gauge. "That's a bit big for a new piercing," I said.

"It doesn't matter. Just do it."

I tugged on some rubber gloves and retrieved the hardware from her creepy little box. "I need to sterilize it."

"No need. It's taken care of." She snapped the box closed

as the dead man in my chair convulsed again. "Besides, there isn't time."

He writhed in the seat and leaned forward with his head between his knees until the spasms stopped. When he sat back, his gaze fixated on my throat. His mouth dropped open and released a soft sigh. I swear he was watching the blood flow in my neck.

While I was eyeing Zombie Man, Creole Lady had produced a set of handcuffs, and by the time I realized what she was doing, she had finished cuffing her friend's hands to the chair. The ratcheting of the cuffs reminded me how much I wanted them out of my shop.

"Hey, now." I raised my hands. "I don't know what you two are into, but I don't do anything weird. Look, maybe we should do this some other time. Your friend here seems real sick, and to be honest, a little creepy. So..."

Creole Lady pulled something else from her purse, then brought it up for me to see. If my mamma told me once, she told me a thousand times, *If it don't feel right, it ain't right.* The small .22-caliber pistol Creole Lady pointed at my nose seemed to echo mamma's sentiment. *Damn, I really should have listened to her more.*

"No more screwing around. Get it done. Now!" she snapped.

It wasn't the first time I've had a gun thrust in my face, but it was the first time I didn't question the gun owner's willingness to use it.

"All right. Where does it go?" I tried to sound cool.

"Left eyebrow will do," she said, gesturing with the gun.

I leaned forward to mark the spot with a pen when Zombie Man suddenly lurched forward with his mouth, snapping at my throat like a rabid dog.

"Jesus! I can't do anything with him bouncing around like that."

Creole Lady seemed to have a moment of indecision. Then,

in an obviously practiced move, she took up position behind the chair and swiftly wrapped her free arm around Zombie Man's neck. With her other hand, she kept the gun aimed at my nose.

"Let's get on with it," she said.

I took up my piercing blade. I pinched the skin above the man's eyebrow and heard a soft fracturing sound like bones snapping. I thought perhaps I had broken something on the frail man, but when I looked down, I couldn't have been more wrong. The noise was coming from his open mouth, and I watched in horror as his canine teeth grew a full inch.

I recoiled. "What the hell is he?"

"Pop, you got less than a minute to get this done or we're both real dead!" Her eyes met mine, and I could see that I wasn't the only one about to piss their pants.

When I heard the bone-splintering sounds again, I tried not to look but couldn't help myself. His mouth had opened wider than humanly possible, and the rest of his jagged ivories were growing. His teeth looked like inmates during a prison break, scattering in all directions—escaping the confinement of his gums.

"Do it!" she screamed.

I reached up for his eyebrow again, and my fingers slipped off. I thought it was the man's sweat that was making him slippery, but I took a closer look.

Hair was growing out of his forehead. It was thin at first, but in seconds it merged with his hairline and became as thick as anyone's scalp.

Then the real noise started. Bone-cracking sounds came from his whole body as he started to reconstruct from the inside out. His mouth pushed forward, becoming a snout barely able to restrain its teeth. The skin on his convulsing fingers splintered and cracked as claws forced their way from the tips, like newborn reptiles bursting through eggshells.

"Do it!" she pleaded.

"I can't even see his eyebrow anymore! Lord, have mercy!"

Diving in, I made a hole somewhere about the eyebrow—or where the eyebrow used to be. As fast as I could, I shoved the unsterilized post in the hole as his teeth snapped at my arm.

The handcuffs broke, and his clawed hand flailed. I backed off my stool, hoping to evade the monster's grasp.

Creole Lady dropped the gun and tried to restrain the thrashing, hair-covered hand. She caught it by the fingers just as the claws and hair started to recede.

After several more violent moments and, God help me, howling, their fingers intertwined, and she pulled his hand back down to the chair's armrest.

The face of the beast withdrew, and in its place was one that resembled a Neanderthal—hairy, oversized cheekbones and a prehistoric brow. In another moment, even those disappeared, sinking back into the normal folds of human expression.

Creole Lady uncuffed the man's other hand.

He stretched like someone waking from a long nap, looking much better than he did when he came in. He looked alive. "Was I a bother?" he said to Creole Lady.

"No, sweetie." She kissed his forehead. "We were running a bit late, that's all. Won't happen again. Promise."

He spun in the chair and looked at himself in the mirror. "Very nice," he said, touching the newly pierced eyebrow.

Creole Lady must have read the confusion that had to be all over my face. "He doesn't have it under control yet. The silver helps." She smiled and turned to her companion. "Let's go. You're on stage in an hour." She dug in her purse again, then stuck a couple of tickets in my shirt pocket. "Come check out the show, Pops."

I recognized the venue from the color of the tickets—a god-awful industrial music club down the street. "No, thanks. I'm a Crosby, Stills, and Nash man."

"Suit yourself," she said, then took her friend by the hand and headed for the door. They left my shop arm in arm. Creole Lady stopped at the entrance and changed my closed sign back to open, then as quickly as they had come, they were gone.

I stared at the reflection of the full moon in the glass of my front window and listened to my heart pound. After my pumping blood returned to its normal rhythm, or as close as it would ever get to normal again, I looked down at the tickets. They read: **One Night Only at The Bone Yard – The Musical Stylings of THE LON CHANEY JUNIORS**.

Yessir, I'll tell you what: this is one tale I won't be telling my grandchildren.

The Lure of Heaven

The voice wound its way through the darkened bedroom, and Karen opened herself to its message. Soothing and gentle in its vibrations, it cradled her in an angelic embrace.

She had heard the same voice in her dreams now for three nights in a row, but this dream seemed more intense than the previous two. More resonant, clearer, it sounded as though the speaker was in the room instead of perched high in the heavens as it had been before.

Only when the voice died away did she grasp why it was different now. This time she was awake. She was sitting up in her bed, arms outstretched toward the ceiling, reaching for heaven. She didn't remember raising her arms, but up until a few moments ago, she also thought she was asleep. Lowering her arms, she felt a warmth so deep that it gave new energy to her spirit. *Thank you, God,* she thought. *Thank you.*

Michael stirred to consciousness. When his eyes finally focused, he saw Karen throwing on clothes. He looked over at the alarm clock: 11:42 p.m.

"Karen," Michael said, "what in God's name are you doing?"

"I understand, Michael. I understand." She pulled on her shoes.

Michael sat up. "Understand what?"

"The dreams," she answered with growing enthusiasm. "Only they're not dreams. At least tonight's wasn't. Maybe the other two weren't either. I don't know. But I know what they mean." Karen moved toward the door.

Not quite awake yet, Michael nonetheless leaped from the bed to prevent his wife's exit. He gently placed his hands on her shoulders and said, "Slow down, Karen. Tell me what you think the dreams mean." He was well aware of Karen's dreams because they had spent the past two days talking of little else.

"They're about understanding. I know now why we never had children." Michael was taken aback, but Karen continued. "All my life, I've known that God had a higher purpose for me. That I was put here to do something for the Lord. We never had children because that would interfere with my true destiny—my calling."

Michael responded in a tender voice. "We never had children because I'm sterile, sweetheart."

"And who made you that way?"

Michael sighed.

"God did," she said. "Remember when we thought that God was punishing us by making us childless? Now I know that it was all part of the plan."

"What plan?"

"God's plan for us, Michael. I've been chosen."

"Chosen for what?"

"To do something divine. To do the Lord's work."

"Can you be a little more specific?"

"I don't know exactly what I'll be doing for the Lord, but I know where it all begins and when."

"Where—and when—is that?"

With determination, Karen said, "Kettlemen's Clearing at midnight. Get dressed. We have fifteen minutes to get there."

Absolute joy radiated from his wife's eyes. He had seen this look before, but never as intense. If Karen believed the Lord wanted her to stomp around in the woods at night, there wasn't a force in heaven or on earth to prevent her from the pilgrimage.

This wouldn't be the first divinely inspired journey for them, but it would be the shortest. Kettleman's Clearing, named for the family that had burned to death in their house on Christmas Eve, was nestled about three hundred yards past a thicket of woods behind their two-story farmhouse. As he had been in the past, Michael was prepared to journey with his wife to wherever her beliefs took them.

Several years ago, when Karen read that a young girl had discovered the image of the Virgin Mary in her cotton candy, they drove ten hours so that Karen could say a prayer over the blessed confection. Last year they flew to Minneapolis to view a bedsheet at a laundromat. It had come out of a dryer with scorch marks that hauntingly resembled the Shroud of Turin.

In both instances, Karen believed she was getting The Calling, but each time she walked away disappointed. Yet that disappointment never shook her faith, not even for a moment. That was one of the things Michael loved about her. Her unshakable devotion to her spirituality, no matter how disappointing it sometimes was, made him feel special just to be around her. On some level, he believed she was blessed.

"Okay," Michael said. "Just give me a minute to put some shoes on. He jumped into his sneakers and pulled his robe off the bathroom door. A minute later, they were carving a path through the woods behind their house, with only a single flashlight to chase away the darkness. Although there was a full moon, a blanket of clouds masked the satellite's full brilliance, reducing it to a soft glow overhead.

"I don't mean to question your interpretation..." Michael bent some tree branches out of Karen's path. "...but why do you believe it was the voice of our Lord calling to you?"

"I wish I could say it's just a feeling I had, but it isn't. Remember when I told you about when I was a little girl? How I died?"

"When you fell through the ice? I remember."

"I was revived after ten minutes underwater, and the only thing I remember is a bright light—a kind of tunnel—and this beautiful angelic voice that spoke to me." Karen stopped and looked intensely at him. "Michael, it was the same voice."

"What exactly did it say?"

"You mean the exact words?"

"Yeah."

"That is why I know the message is divine because it never uses words. Only meaning. It's like music playing in your head. No words. Just understanding." Karen started walking again and picked up the pace.

Michael fell in line behind her. "I guess I don't understand why God wants us to go to a clearing where people died on the anniversary eve of our Savior's birth... and in the middle of the night."

"I don't have that answer, Michael, but I do know that all will be revealed and our true purpose made clear. I've received The Calling, and as my husband, you must walk with me on this path to God's greater glory." They emerged from the woods into Kettelmen's Clearing.

The clearing was about a hundred yards in diameter, with all that remained of the Kettlemen's house, a concrete foundation, resting dead center. Arising from the foundation were two fire-scarred chimneys. Karen hurried to the remnants of the

Kettlemen's house as Michael looked around with suspicion.

They met at the center of the foundation, about where the Kettlemen's kitchen and dining room would have been forty years ago. Michael asked, "What now?"

"I don't know."

Why was she now uncertain? Up to this point, she had been so positive about everything. But before Michael could respond, he heard a twig snap in the distance. Michael whirled around and peered into the darkness. Karen pointed the flashlight in the direction of Michael's gaze.

"You heard that, right?" Michael's voice trembled.

"Yes. What was it?"

Snapping twigs and the shuffling of feet echoed in the trees. It seemed to come from the woods on the opposite side of their entrance. It was growing louder. It was coming closer.

"Can you see anything?" he said.

"No. God, Michael, what is it?"

"I don't know." As Michael looked around for a weapon, a shape took form in the darkness. It lumbered under great weight and staggered through the thicket. On either side of the robust silhouette, two smaller creatures crawled through the woods, sometimes on all fours and sometimes walking erect.

"What the...?" Michael looked back at his wife. Their eyes met, and for a moment, he didn't know whether they should fight or flee. Before they reached a decision, a woman's voice spoke.

"Hello." A middle-aged woman, a stout figure with two children in tow, emerged from the trees.

Karen squinted. "It's Anne Carson and her two boys."

"Who?"

"Anne Carson. She plays the organ at church." Attending an evangelical church the size of the one Michael and Karen went to made it impossible to know every member. Karen recognized most of the members and knew many by name, but

Anne was not one she knew personally.

Karen lit the path with the flashlight for the new arrivals as they moved toward the foundation. Michael gave the round woman a hand, helping her onto the foundation, and then escorted her and the boys to where Karen stood. The conversation was fast. Karen and Michael learned that Anne had the same dreams and received the same instruction. And like Karen, she believed the message to be divine.

"I brought my boys along 'cause... Well, I couldn't leave them home alone. What would the Lord think of me then?" She smiled between pudgy cheeks. "I just wish I had thought enough ahead to bring a flashlight."

The boys couldn't be much older than eight or ten. They looked tired and confused. Tromping through the woods in the dark had rattled them a bit, perhaps, but they seemed unharmed.

"Michael." Karen aimed the flashlight into the thicket where Anne and her boys had emerged. Soft lights flickered through the trees. About half a dozen flashlights were cutting a path through the woods. In a few minutes, people began to emerge.

Karen's face had lost some of its earlier glow. It was the kind of thing that only a husband would notice. And he did. He put his arm around her.

"I'm sorry," he said.

"For what?"

"You thought you were The One—the *only* one—chosen."

"That would be selfish. God punishes the selfish," Karen said.

"The Lord needs many shepherds to tend his flock, and you're so lucky to have been chosen to be one." He hoped this encouraged her. Karen smiled and embraced him as the first of the newcomers mounted the blackened foundation.

It was an amazing assemblage of individuals. Only the most righteous and God-fearing, representing several different faiths, had been summoned. Father Mitchell, from Our Lady of the Divine Embrace, was there, along with Rabbi Gordon from the county's synagogue. The nation of Islam was represented by Mr. and Mrs. Nashiri. Twenty-eight in all had made the journey, either encouraged by the heavenly voice or from association with someone who had heard it. Conversations moved through the crowd like a snake through the grass.

"I thought when I heard The Calling for the first time as a teenager that I'd been touched by the hand of God. But it was never as clear as it was tonight," announced Father Mitchell. Sounds of acknowledgment moved around the group.

"I agree," Rabbi Gordon said while smiling at his good friend and theological rival. "There is no question that Yahweh has brought us to this place."

"Glory be to God," someone said from the back.

"But why?" Michael asked.

Faces, illuminated only by flashlights, turned and scowled at him as if he had said something blasphemous. Karen stepped in front of him. "Forgive him. He did not hear the Lord's voice. I did."

Expressions of understanding moved through the group, and Father Mitchell spoke to Michael. "We've all received The Calling, and it told us our true purpose is going to be revealed. A purpose that will be for the glory of God. And since you have journeyed to this Holy place, I'm sure the Lord wants you to do his bidding as well." Father Mitchell seemed to be taking over as leader of the group. Something he was accustomed to doing. "Everyone," he said, "let us join hands and pray."

With excitement, everyone formed a circle, grasping the hands of those on either side. Karen looked at Michael and smiled. "It won't be long now. I can feel it."

"O Lord, my God," Father Mitchell began, "Creator and Ruler of the universe, it is Your will that human beings accept the duty of work. May the task You have selected these chosen few to undertake bring growth in this life and to those we love and help to extend the Kingdom..."

His words trailed off as a ray of light descended from the night sky, taking everyone by surprise. Father Mitchell turned his gaze heavenward, as did others, and continued the prayer, his voice rising. "Give these Chosen Ones work that draws them to You and to each other in cheerful service. We unite in duty with sacrifice so that it may be pleasing to You and give You glory."

Father Mitchell's words continued in the background as Michael and Karen stared at the clouds overhead, so thick a minute ago but now parting like the Red Sea. The light descended through the expanding breach in the clouds, and its narrow beam touched down in the middle of the circle. Gasps of excitement exploded as the beam, a golden ray of circular luminescence, began to expand, moving toward the Chosen Ones. In less than a minute, the heavenly glow had encompassed them all. It felt warm and inviting.

Before Michael could fully enjoy the warmth, a new sensation tingled deep inside him. Small at first, but within a heartbeat, it spread throughout the body. It was a feeling of weightlessness, not just of mass, but of burden, anxiety, and the need to question. Euphoria consumed him, and he scarcely noticed that his feet had left the ground. The circle of Chosen Ones was rising.

As some looked down, watching the ground fall away, a cold realization materialized on their faces. They were now all marionettes who knew very little about the puppet master. Panic started to spread, and the circle severed in a dozen places.

Attempting to quell the screams, Father Mitchell's voice rose to a shout. "We beg Your blessing upon all our efforts and ask that You lead us to our work. With the one true God as our shepherd, help us do the work You have asked and come to the reward You have prepared!"

Michael looked at Karen and saw that she was not afraid. She grabbed Michael's free hand and pulled him close to her.

"It's going to be all right, Michael. Just have faith." Her smile was as blissful as the day they'd met. "Have faith."

Karen believed enough for both of them. Michael let go of all fear and felt himself fill with unending joy. "I love you," he said as they continued to drift heavenward. They held each other and let the power of their faith carry them away.

Just after dawn, Anne Carson's two boys drifted out of unconsciousness as thick morning fog glided through Kettlemen's Clearing. The older of the two got to his feet first, stumbled slightly, then righted himself. Seeing his younger sibling struggling to sit up, he bent down and said, "Are you all right?"

The younger boy wiped his eyes. "I think so. Where's mamma?"

The oldest looked around. It was only then that he realized they were all alone. "I don't know," he said. "Come on, get up."

As the two made their way back through the woods from which they had come, the youngest boy asked, "Do you think God didn't want us? Were we bad?"

Chief Operations Officer Rallec swam along the main corridor of the Inock Survey and Exploratory vessel as it prepared to break away from the remote solar system's gravitational pull. The staff meeting he called was the final administrative task he had to do before they started the long journey home, and he was eager to get past it. He swam through the hard water door and entered the briefing room. Taking his place on a piece of furniture that served as a chair for his species, he brought a webbed tentacle down on the table, bringing the meeting to order. A dozen attendees went through the topics systematically, and within a short time, they had reached the final point on the agenda—Secured Inventory.

When Supply Officer Balleo announced the topic, Rallec's interest grew. In a language resembling whale song, he asked, "How did the Automated Herding System function this time?"

"Very well," said Balleo. "I think with some minor adjustments, it will be a real asset to deep space exploration. We were able to herd twenty-eight small-brained bipeds to a remote location and secure them without disrupting the environment."

"Interesting," Rallec declared with genuine regard. "I'm still not clear on how it works."

"It analyzes a civilization, and based on the findings, it crafts a message that the animals would find so alluring, so commanding, they will not even question it. The message varies from planet to planet. After a time, the message becomes a beacon, and this herds the animals to a specific location," Balleo explained.

"Fascinating." Rallec glanced down at his data shell. "But I see a discrepancy in your haul. You said you herded twenty-eight bipeds, but only twenty-six were taken aboard."

"Even in this remote end of the galaxy, we are still bound by the Harvesting of Alien Species Limitations Act," Balleo said. "Two of the animals were underweight. Most likely due to age. They were thrown back."

Sounds of disapproval moved through the room as Rallec raised a tentacle. "Now, now. It is reasonable to have harvesting limitations. If there weren't, then there might not be enough bipeds for the next Inocks who come this way. We have twenty-six healthy adult animals, which should last us 'til we reach Alben Five. Now, speaking of dinner, when will they be ready?"

"Soon," Balleo said. "I saw several of the animals being deboned in the galley on my swim over."

"Excellent," Rallec said, rubbing a tentacle over three of his six stomachs. "I'm so hungry I could eat one of my wives."

The Mount of Death

"Beer me!"

Collin took a hand off the steering wheel, the one not holding his smartphone, and thrust it back toward Aaron.

Aaron shifted uncomfortably in the SUV's rear compartment, wedged between a cooler and sleeping bags. It was the only spot left since Collin and his girlfriend occupied the front, and Max and Carole took up the entire backseat.

"Not gonna happen. You're driving—and texting," Aaron replied. *And a colossal douche*, he wanted to add but didn't. Collin's sober driving on the treacherous, heavily forested Highway 39 through the San Gabriele Mountains was scary enough. There wasn't a chance in hell Aaron would allow alcohol into the mix.

"Hey, I'm not going to spend the weekend in the woods with you people, sober," Collin said. "Now, beer me."

Max leaned forward on the back of the driver's seat and slapped Collin's shoulder. "Love you, too, buddy."

Collin rolled his entire head. "Ahh, I didn't mean it like... For the love of... Aaron, will you please just get me a damn beer."

Collin's new girlfriend—Aaron couldn't remember her name... Debbie... Donna... something—turned from the passenger seat window and smiled at Aaron. "I'll take a Coke."

Aaron narrowed his gaze at the young woman he felt answered the age-old question, *What would a Wookie look like if it lost all its hair?*, then started looking for a Coke.

Max reached back and put his hand on the cooler lid. "Got a Red Bull back there?"

Aaron furrowed his brow. "When did I become the bartender?"

Collin drummed his fingers impatiently on the roof. "When you volunteered to sit in the ass-end of the car."

Volunteered? Everyone had simply beaten him to the car. Aaron sighed. Who was he kidding? It made sense that he was tucked in with the luggage. He was the fifth wheel, Max's best friend. Collin had Debbie or Donna or whatever the hell Wookie-face's name was, and Max had Carole.

God, Carole was amazing. Beautiful, strong, intelligent. She had the brains of Dana Scully, the eyes of Deanna Troi, and the tenacity of Katniss Everdeen. Her hair rested over the back-seat right in front of Aaron, and he delighted in every breath he took, filling his nostrils with her fragrance: clean, fresh, with a hint of strawberry. He was well aware of how creepy it was, but it wasn't like he could move or find some other air to breathe.

"Hey, you awake?" Collin shouted. "Look, I'm putting my phone down. Now, beer-me."

Max slapped Collin's hand down off the roof. "Crystal Lake Campgrounds is less than an hour away. Just wait."

Collin put his hand back up, wrist resting against the soft top and fingers shaped as if cradling a beer. "I want to be well into my first buzz by then. Now tell Comic-Con back there to get me a beer."

"Collin!" Aaron sat up. "You vomit-spackled ninja-fart, I'm not getting you a beer. You can barely drive sober in the light of day, let alone in the dark. Jesus, man, it's pitch-black out."

Collin made a wide sweeping gesture over the dashboard. "Aaron, my nerdy little friend, there is nothing out there in the dark that ain't there in the daytime."

"That's some brilliant fortune cookie wisdom there, Buddha," Aaron shouted.

Max turned around. "Dude, that sounded kind of racist."

"What? No, that's not—"

"I could use a Seven-up or something like that," Carole said, turning around, temporarily paralyzing Aaron with the full power of her deep brown Deanna Troi eyes.

"Yeah, I'll see what I can...uh..." Aaron looked away and plunged his attention into the cooler.

When he looked back up, Max was staring at him, uneasy. He seemed to be reading something on Aaron's face. Something Aaron had been trying to bury for months. Although he hadn't done anything disloyal to his friend, Aaron knew it was more from a lack of opportunity than an unwillingness to do so.

Max brought his arm up and slid it around Carole's shoulder, pulling her close.

Shit. Aaron turned away and continued rummaging through the cold cans. The weight of the guilt for something he hadn't even done yet crushed him. He and Max had been close since third grade, ever since they discovered their mutual interest in all things geeky, especially Science Fiction. Truth be known, Max was a little more *Star Wars* than *Star Trek*, but Aaron felt that when it came to best friends, certain things can be forgiven. They cosplayed at conventions together; they joined a quidditch league together; they even went to their prom together. Not *with* each other. There were girls involved. The point being, they were tight. At least until Max started playing lacrosse and hanging out with troglodytes like Collin and his Wookie-faced girlfriend. Aaron felt them drift apart over the past year, and now he was falling for Max's girlfriend, a circumstance guaranteed not to improve the situation.

Collin turned down the rap music he'd insisted on tormenting his passengers with since San Bernardino, and then he cleared his throat, clearly wanting everyone's attention.

"Allow me to demonstrate," Collin said.

Demonstrate what?

There was a soft click, and the car plunged into darkness.

"What the...?" Aaron let the cooler lid fall and turned forward, unable to see the curvy road or the surrounding trees. In the driver's seat, Collin's hands, illuminated by the faint glow of dashboard lights, waved in the air like someone reaching the top of the big drop on a roller coaster.

Max slapped Collin in the back of the head. "Turn the headlights back on, asshole!"

Collin's hands lowered. There was a click, and the lights came back on.

Aaron's hands were shaking. "Seriously! Is there any part of you that's not stupid?"

Collin's grin reflected in the rearview mirror. "Just conducting a little science experiment about the dark."

"Well, congratulations," Aaron said. "You proved you're a moron."

Collin raised his hand, once again thrusting it back toward Aaron, fingers cradling an invisible beer can. "I told ya there ain't nothing there in the dark that isn't there in the daylight. Now stop being a Beer-Nazi or I'll conduct another experiment."

Collin's girlfriend turned around. "Yeah, stop being a Beer-Nazi."

Aaron pointed a finger. "Nobody is talking to you, Donna."

"My name is DeeDee, you skid-mark."

"Whatever," Aaron said. "Collin, when we get to Crystal Lake, you can drink yourself into a coma. But let's get there alive." Aaron raised his right hand. "All in favor?"

Carole and Max raised their hands.

Collin shook his head. "Well, this isn't a democracy."

Soft click.

Darkness swallowed the landscape, and Aaron's entire body began to tremble. "You shit-head!"

In a casual tone, Collin said, "Beer me."

"All right," Aaron said. "Just turn them on."

"Another successful experiment." Collin flicked the head-lights back on.

White light illuminated something in the road. Aaron only caught a glimpse of it. It stood on four legs and had metallic eyeshine the shade of gunmetal. In a horrifying instant, Aaron realized they were going to hit it. The full weight of Thor's hammer seemed to crash down on the hood. Everything rushed forward to the sounds of breaking glass, skidding tires, deploying airbags, and screaming. Ice from the cooler rose, hung in the air, then showered down like Texas hail. Aaron tumbled over the backseat, unable to give any resistance, as cold cans of soda and beer pummeled his back.

He careened into an un-seatbelted Max, and they both slid to the floor in a tangle of limbs. Collin's rap music sadistically rose in volume like background music to a bad horror film as Aaron struggled to right himself in the dark. With arms and legs flailing all around him, he grasped something soft.

Realizing it was some part of Carole, he quickly let go as the SUV slid sideways. He braced for another impact with either a huge, hundred-year-old pine tree or one of the colossal boulders that dotted the roadside. But it didn't come.

The sound of sliding tires suddenly silenced as the vehicle jolted to a stop. One or more doors had buckled enough to turn on the interior lights, and Aaron looked down and saw his feet floating in the air. His blood felt as if it were flowing in the wrong direction; then he realized he wasn't looking down. He was looking up.

"Carole," Max said. "You all right?"

"Yeah, I think."

"Aaron, you alive?" Max said.

Aaron thought about that for a second. The cold rubber of the floor mat pressing against his face indicated that he was. "Guess so."

"Then how about getting your ass-cheeks out of my face?" Max said.

Aaron felt Max's hands clasp his belt, lifting him like a crane. He flopped back into the rear compartment. He then tried to look outside, but most of the view through the front windshield was blocked by the deployed airbags. The view to either side of Max and Carole was also obstructed by airbags.

A head rose from the front seat, hair in disarray. Collin's girlfriend moaned, touching a finger to her bruised forehead.

"Debbie, are you okay," Aaron said, bringing out a pocket-knife.

She moaned again. "My name is DeeDee, you ass-wipe."

Aaron sighed. "She's fine." He flipped open the blade and handed the knife up to Max. "Hey, Collin?"

There was no movement from the driver's seat. Max plunged the blade into the backseat airbag to his side; a soft whistling sound filled the car. He reached out and put a hand on Collin's shoulder. "Hey, man."

Collin grunted like a gorilla fighting to wake from a nap. His head flopped to one side. "Feels like there's something sitting on me," Collin said. "Can't feel my legs."

Everyone sat still for a few moments. Collin's heavy breathing was the only opposition to silence.

Aaron glanced over at Max, who seemed to take a deep breath, then said, "Okay, let's stay calm. Carole, call nine-one-one."

"I'm on it." Carole began digging for her phone.

Max handed the knife back to Aaron, then opened his door.

Aaron grabbed Max's shoulder. "Where're you going?"

"I'm gonna check out the car. You stay here with DeeDee and see what you can do for Collin." Max stepped out.

Aaron lowered his voice. "Why me?"

Max stuck his head back in, extending a hand toward Carole. "Cuz you're studying to be a doctor."

"I want to be a biologist."

Max cocked his head. "What's the difference?"

Carole slid across the backseat to follow. Before stepping out, she whispered to Aaron, "I know the difference."

Aaron took a moment to watch her leave, then hopped into the backseat to take a look at Collin while his girlfriend pushed on the steering wheel.

"Donna, what're you doing?"

She stopped, glancing over at Aaron. "It's De—oh, never-the-fuck-mind. Just help me."

"Let's get this out of the way first," Aaron said, stabbing the muffin top-shaped airbag that had deployed from the steering wheel. As the bag deflated, Aaron leaned into the front seat and looked into Collin's lap. The entire steering column was bent downward, pressing into Collin's stomach. "Aaron," Collin said. "Can you see my legs? I think I'm stuck."

Aaron put a hand on Collin's shoulder, peering down.

"Everything's gonna be okay. Help is coming. Just hang—"

"I can't move, man?"

Below Collin's knees, Aaron couldn't see anything. The area around the pedals was completely caved in. Whatever they had struck must have been solid and very heavy. "You're pinned in real good," Aaron said, trying to muster up some genuine concern for a guy he couldn't stand, the same guy whose dumbass antics had caused this mess. "I don't think you're getting out without help."

"Jeez, my head hurts." Collin touched a golf ball-sized welt on his forehead.

Aaron eyed the lump. "Are you dizzy, tired, nauseous?"

"Yes, yes, and more yes," Collin said.

The door of the rear compartment swung open. Aaron snapped around, saw Max riffling through the luggage. "What's going on?"

Max held up a finger. "Not now." He pulled out a flashlight and shut the door.

What the hell? What could be so damn important that Max didn't have time to answer? *And why the hell am I in here taking care of his idiotic friend?*

Collin's girlfriend raised a hand, pushing the front passenger-side airbag away from her face.

Aaron leaned forward with his pocketknife up. "Let me get that."

"No, I got it." She pulled a nail file out of her purse and stabbed the bag. It deflated in a few seconds.

Aaron looked at Collin, noticing his usually smug expression was slightly less smug.

"Aaron," Max called from outside. "Get out here."

"You need to stay awake," Aaron said as Collin let his head flop back onto the headrest.

"How about just a little nap," Collin mumbled.

Max's voice came again from right behind Aaron. "Aaron, I really need you to see this."

Aaron turned and looked at Max. "What?"

Max made an insistent gesture with the flashlight, then stepped away.

Aaron turned forward and met DeeDee's eyes. "Look, keep him awake, and I'll be right..." His words faded as he glimpsed the windshield. A spider web of white cracks filled the glass, but not enough to obscure his vision. Something else lying on the hood was doing that.

Is that hair, Aaron thought? *And that looks like a...a saddle.*

"I'm gonna step out for a minute," Aaron said. "I'll be back."

Aaron hopped out, following the line of Max's flashlight

illuminating Carole standing a good distance down the road, her smartphone pressed to her ear.

"What's she doing way over there?" Aaron asked.

Max turned around, his face lit eerily by the vehicle's only working headlight. "That's as close as she wants to get to this thing." He waved at Carole, and she returned it with a nod, then Max aimed the flashlight at the hood.

Aaron's mouth dropped open, and he instinctively stepped back. In a kind of perplexed daze, he joined Max standing just a few feet in front of the bumper.

"What the hell is that?" Aaron said.

"You tell me," Max said.

"Is..." Aaron stepped forward, fascination beginning to over-ride his initial horror. "Is it a horse?"

Max moved the light toward the bumper, illuminating the thing's feet. "Do horses have toes?"

"Not lately," Aaron said. "Shine the light on its back."

The beam drifted up the creature's dark, alien exterior. Its underbelly was gaunt, leathery, and disturbingly unfamiliar.

And then Aaron saw something that was at least a little familiar. "That looks like a saddle."

Max's head tilted a bit. "Are you sure that's a saddle, City Boy?"

"According to all the John Wayne movies I've seen, that's a saddle." Aaron held out his hand. "Give me that."

Max handed him the flashlight, and Aaron brought it up over his head, aiming the beam down, illuminating the creature's entire form. "Jesus," Aaron breathed.

"What the hell is this?" Max said.

Aaron shook his head, taking in the enigma sprawled out on the hood. Its form resembled a horse, but that is where the comparison ended. Instead of hooves, the thing had muscular, three-toed feet, each toe encased in a predator's claw, wide and jagged, stained in an array of colors from bone white to deep crimson. The equine frame was covered with short hair that glistened in the flashlight beam like rows of staples. A tail dangled off the hood by the front tire, comprised of hundreds of thick, rust-colored, and somewhat familiar strands. Aaron stepped closer, wanting to touch the tail and confirm the image his mind must have been imagining.

At the last moment, he thought better of it and settled for shining the light on it and gazing at the strands.

Is... Is the tail made of barbed wire?

"Damn," Max said. "Shine the light over here. Look at these teeth."

Aaron redirected the beam to the creature's head, which lay on the roof; its lips receded along the protracted snout in an unsettling death grin. The light bounced off and through the teeth, giving Aaron the impression that the fangs were icicles frozen to its black gums. But as he moved the light back and forth, he realized that the long, spike-shaped teeth were transparent, as if made from glass or crystal.

"What the fu..." Max said, moving away from the beast's head. "This can't be real. Right?"

Aaron was about to answer, but he'd moved the light down the thing's neck, and his words caught in his throat. Protruding from the spot where a normal horse would have a mane of hair were thick slimy follicles, with ungodly ridges spiraling around each strand. They, too, had an unnerving ring of familiarity. The beast's mane seemed made of a thousand dead, oversized earthworms.

"I don't know what's creeping me out more," Max said. "The fact that I'm really looking at this...or that someone actually rides this thing."

"Could be pre-historic," Aaron said, moving around to its head.

Carole's voice cut through the dark. "You mean like a dinosaur?"

Aaron aimed the light at Carole, now standing just behind Max. "Not exactly." He gestured to her phone. "What'd they say?"

She rolled her brown eyes. "No one can get here for at least a half-hour, maybe longer. And my battery just died."

"Jeez," Aaron said.

Max pointed to the front seat. "How's Collin?"

"He has a slight concussion; I'm guessing not his first. He's dizzy and stuck under the steering column. This thing caved in the area around his legs. He's pinned tight, and he isn't getting free until they can get here and cut him out."

"But he'll be all right?" Max said.

"Yeah. I mean, he'll still be Collin, but aside from that, as long as what's-her-face keeps him awake, he'll be fine."

"Is there anything we could do to help him while we wait?" Carole said.

Aaron shrugged. "I guess we could get this thing off him. Max, get its tail."

"You nuts? I ain't touching this thing."

Aaron shined the light on his friend. "It's dead."

"How do you know?" Max said.

"We just hit it with a two-ton car." Aaron turned the beam on the creature's defined ribcage, visible under hair-covered flesh. "It isn't breathing."

Max walked toward the creature's tail. "We don't even know if it needs to breathe. It might be from outer space or another time. Or it could be a robot, even."

Aaron shined the light on Max's face. "Dude, no more SyFy channel for you?"

Max gazed down, clearly fascinated. "Man, just look at this thing."

Aaron turned his attention to the creature's head. Its face seemed too long for a horse, almost a foot too long, and its snout seemed to be designed for tearing meat from bone rather than grassing in a field. He found the thing's closed eyes and placed a thumb across one eyelid. Through the thin layer of skin, he could feel that the eye underneath was ridged, not spherical or smooth. He pushed the lid up. There was a suction sound like someone pulling a shoe out of the mud.

He aimed the flashlight. The thing's eyeball wasn't an eyeball at all, but a small human skull cast from gray metal, like the kind of ring decoration found on the finger of a Hell's Angel. "Ah, crap-weasel," Aaron said, letting the eyelid fall closed and stepping back.

"What is it?" Max said, his voice noticeably elevated.

Aaron staggered backward, the flashlight still aimed at the thing's face. He took a breath. "Just reconsidering your alien, time-traveling robot theory." He looked up at Max. "I don't think we should move it."

Collin's girlfriend stuck her head out the window, placing a hand on the creature's rump. "Hey, what is this?"

Max stepped forward and removed her hand. "Be careful. Maybe... Don't touch it."

She recoiled. "Okay."

"How's Collin?" Max asked, standing just behind the thing's back legs.

She sighed. "He keeps trying to nod off."

"Well, help is on the way," Aaron said. "So keep his eyes open."

She delivered a salute. "Yes, Sir, Captain Douchebag," then disappeared back into the car.

Aaron chuckled. "I might be starting to like her."

"There's no accounting for taste," Max said, then glanced down at the creature. He took a step closer, holding his hands above the thing as if it were a warm fire. "Hey, Aaron."

"What?"

"Do you think it's worth something?"

Aaron furrowed his brow.

"I mean, it's gotta be one of a kind, right?" Max sounded excited. "A couple of months back, there was this three-headed dog that went for ten-thousand on eBay. Hell, this thing could beat that, easy."

Aaron rolled his eyes.

"I'm talking even split," Max said. "You, me, Carole, Collin, and even what's-her-name." Max grinned. "So?"

"So, what?" Aaron said.

"What do you think we could get for it?"

"I don't know, Max. My market knowledge of pre-historic alien, time-traveling robot horses is a bit limited. Besides, I think you're forgetting one minor detail."

"What's that?"

Carole pointed to the creature's back. "The saddle."

"Exactly," Aaron said. "Someone or something owns this... whatever it is. And I'm not particularly interested in meeting—" Aaron's words stuck in his throat as his blood suddenly turned cold. His eyes went wide, so wide they felt as if they would pop from their sockets. "Max."

"What?"

"Get away from it."

"Why?"

"Now." Aaron took a step back, his gaze locked on the creature's face. The eyeball-sized human skulls were wide open. Aaron heard several soft pings, like metal moving through air. He glanced down. Steak knife-sized claws extended from the creature's hind legs like rear hallux talons on a bird of prey.

"Max, get back," Aaron shouted. "It's not dead."

Max took a step, but it wasn't big enough. All four of the thing's legs kicked out as it tried to get up. The back leg talons slashed across Max's mid-section, and he went down.

Aaron rushed around the car, meeting Carole at Max's side.

Max tried to sit up, his hands clasped around his abdomen.

Aaron aimed the flashlight at his midsection. Blood poured between Max's fingers.

Max glanced down, then back up at Aaron. "It really hurts."

Aaron handed Carole the flashlight and grabbed Max under the armpit.

"It's just a scratch," Carole said, taking Max's other side. "Stop acting like a girl."

Max smiled for a second, then pain seemed to erase the expression, like chalk from a blackboard. They lifted Max to his feet while Max kept one hand fixed on his abdomen. He seemed to be pushing as if struggling to keep things inside.

They dragged Max to the side of the road, Aaron fighting the urge to look back even as he heard Collin and DeeDee begin to scream. Max pushed Carole ahead toward the forest and said, "Run."

Carole hesitated, looking back at the boys, but then she glanced over their shoulders and clearly saw something. Something horrible. Her mouth fell open, her eyes bulged, and even in the thin moonlight, Aaron could see her tremble. "Just go," Max said. "Run!"

Carole spun on a heel and darted into the forest. The sound of bone and talons scraping on metal echoed behind them, and Aaron and Max paused to look back.

The horse-creature had righted itself and was now standing on the hood. The SUV's back wheels were several inches off the ground, teetering like a seesaw on the front axle. Collin's girlfriend screamed, looking up through the windshield, hands clamped tight on the dashboard. Her shrill, terrified screams seemed to be aggravating the creature. The angular snout arched upward, and each hair in its mane moved under its own momentum like the venomous strands on Medusa's head.

Aaron took a step toward the car but felt Max's hand around his shoulder, holding him.

With mouth open and transparent teeth glistening in the moonlight, the creature's head darted forward into the windshield like a predatory bird diving into the water. Glass shattered, and the whole car shook.

DeeDee's screams stopped.

The creature pulled its head back out, something round and fleshy stuck in its teeth. Snapping its jaw shut, the thing began to swallow. Aaron saw the outline of the girl's head moving down a long, gaunt throat.

"I told her I'd be right back," Aaron said.

"You lied, man," Max said. "Now let's go."

Using the bouncing light from Carole's flashlight as a beacon, they pursued her into the forest. They hobbled in a clumsy entanglement of limbs, but even terribly wounded, Max seemed the more coordinated of the two.

Before they lost sight of the road, Aaron looked back to see if the horror was following. It wasn't. The beast stood on the hood, slowly sinking into the engine as unimaginable weight pulled it toward the ground.

Instead of getting down, the creature stood up on its hind legs and reared a monstrous head way back. The chest looked to be expanding as if taking in an enormous breath, like a mythical dragon preparing to breathe...

Fire erupted from the beast's mouth as the creature thrust forward. Flames engulfed the car's interior, and smoke and ash exploded through the rear window.

"What was that?" Max said.

Aaron jerked him forward. "Keep going!"

A tree limb smacked Aaron in the face as they crashed through the brush. Carole's bouncing light moved further away.

Max moaned, and his head slumped forward. Aaron felt the pull of his friend's full weight, and they both tumbled to the ground. Aaron landed on top of his friend, their lips close to touching.

Max pushed Aaron off. "Not even if you were pretty and made of money." He grimaced, shutting his eyes.

Aaron got to his knees. "Don't flatter yourself." He grabbed Max's arm. "Now walk it off, you big pie-hole."

Max pulled his arm away, falling flat on the ground. "I appreciate the words of encouragement, but I don't think..."

He pulled his hand away from his stomach briefly. Aaron tried to mask his horror. "I think I'm done."

Both of them sat still, breathing heavily. Aaron looked away.

Max lifted his head. "I'm slowing you down."

Before Aaron could respond, he felt something: a rhythmic vibration stemming from the ground, coursing through his body like precision lighting, striking his flesh first, and then going deeper to rattle his bones. A thunderous echo was just a step behind the vibrations, galloping through the trees. Getting closer. Coming fast.

"What is that?" Aaron said.

"You know what it is," Max said softly. "Aaron, go. Catch Carole."

"Knock off the hero shit," Aaron said, pulling at Max's arm.

Max yanked his arm away, sitting up. "I'll slow it down the best I can."

"Max."

"Just go," Max said, reaching for a broken tree limb.

Aaron stood up. "Max, I—"

"Please don't say anything weird, man. Just go." Max's eyes locked on Aaron's. "Keep her safe, or so help me, I'll find a way back and kick your ass."

Aaron turned away from his friend and ran after Carole. The beam from the flashlight was at least a hundred yards deeper into the forest, blinking as it passed behind trees and bushes, fading from view. He was in danger of losing sight of her. He pushed himself harder. His chest pounded, sweat flowed, his lungs ached, and his legs screamed, *No more.* He wished at some point in his life that he'd taken up running or jogging or any other kind of exercise.

Tree branches slapped at Aaron's body as he ran faster than he knew he could. The smell of pine filled his nose, and he felt his face beginning to rub raw from the scraping of needles. A pinecone hit him square in the forehead, and he slowed to shake it off. He blinked his eyes a few times, then the sound of a bonfire igniting with far too much accelerant boomed behind him. He looked back just in time to see a fireball in the distance ascend into the underside of the forest canopy. Max screamed.

Aaron started running again. The bouncing light ahead was less than a hundred feet away, and he was closing the gap. When he could see her thin silhouette, he called out.

Carole stopped and aimed the beam back at him.

Aaron held up a hand to block the light. "Turn that off."

"Why?"

"You're like a freakin' lighthouse."

"Where's Max?"

"He...he went a different way."

"He did what?"

"He's trying to keep it off our tail." Aaron pushed her forward. "Go, go."

She turned toward him, defiant. "How is he going to keep it..."

Her words faded, and sadness flickered in her eyes as understanding washed over her features. Aaron shook his head. "There's no time for this." He grabbed her wrist and pulled as he started to move. She resisted for only a moment. Then they ran in the dark, stumbling every few yards. Aaron fell twice, and Carole stopped each time, pulling him to his feet. After several more minutes, Carole smacked into a tree and tumbled backward. Aaron hit the same damn tree and fell across her legs.

Crap. Aaron rolled off her, feeling the damp needles covering the ground beneath him. "You okay?"

"Yeah. Need to rest."

"Just for a few..." Aaron breathed deeply, lying flat on the ground. Fear-induced adrenaline flowed through him, but he could do nothing with it. It was fuel for a machine that was grossly out of shape, and all it did was cause his head to pound, his limbs to shake, and a wave of displaced nausea to move into parts of his body he wasn't aware could even feel nausea. A part of him wanted this to be over. Just let it end. But another part, the part that was focusing on the distant vibrations in the earth bearing down on them like a herd of buffalo, had another idea. Embrace the adrenaline. Aaron sprang to his feet. "Break's over."

"Just a few more..." Carole began to say but stopped as a distant galloping began to resonate through the trees. "I'm ready." Carole jumped up and took off running, leaving Aaron standing still.

Soon Aaron was on her heels again, the galloping growing louder behind them. Aaron knew it was his imagination, but he swore he felt the thing breathing on his collar. He slapped at the rising hairs on the back of his neck, dirt and sweat running down his shirt.

The galloping was so close now; it couldn't be more than ten or twenty yards behind them—thunderous, pounding.

Carole turned hard to the right and ducked at the base of a wide tree. Aaron joined her, tucking in behind it, and they cowered at the tree's base, one of many that lined a small, oval-shaped clearing where only moss-covered boulders and dead pine needles littered the ground.

The galloping stopped. The forest went still for a moment; nothing moved, nothing breathed. Carole put a trembling hand over her mouth.

Something moved by fast; forest debris caught in the enormous wake showered down in a rain of dirt, bark, and pine needles. As the debris settled, Carole and Aaron stood up slowly, each having a tight grip on the other.

"Where'd it go?" Carole whispered.

High above, a tree branch snapped in the distance. Then another. Then a symphony of breaking limbs sounded. Aaron looked up but couldn't accept what he saw. The creature was above them, moving within the forest canopy like a snake through grass, defying gravity, reason, and sanity. Branches and pine-cones hit the forest floor with echoing thuds, forcing Aaron to believe.

Then the trees went quiet, needles continuing to float down in the silence.

They looked at each other, Aaron's nose inches from Carole's. "I think it's gone," he said.

Carole breathed deep. "What the hell is that—"

The ground shook, sending a tremor through Aaron's body.

The four-legged beast straightened up ten feet in front of them. Enormous, leathery, black wings slowly folded to its side, tucking just beneath the saddle. The creature blinked and jos-tled a fire-breathing head. The hairs on an animated mane floated all around as if submerged underwater, giving life to each tendril. Teeth bared, the thing reared up on hind legs, and the already broad chest expanded to the sound of air in-haled down the gullet.

"What's it doing?" Carole said, her nails digging into Aaron's back.

Aaron put a hand on her chin, pulling her face toward him. "Don't look, okay." He closed his eyes, resolute that after a few painful moments it would all be over. "Sorry, Max."

A wave of cold rushed by, icy, biting. Aaron opened his eyes.

A towering figure stood with its back to them, a dark cloak shrouding it from head to foot.

"Take it easy, my friend," the cloaked figure said in a deep and hollow voice.

In one hand, the figure held a macabre-looking bridle. Aaron narrowed his eyes. There was something wrong with its hands. They were extremely bony. No, not bony. They were bone.

"Please excuse my pet," the newcomer said, sliding the bridle around the creature's snout. "He's naturally very curious about your world." The skeletal hand reached into its cloak, pulled out a pile of something worm-like, fleshy, and placed it under the creature's mouth. "He wanders off whenever he gets the chance. Don't you, boy?"

Aaron watched as the creature began to feed on the pile of nightcrawlers and maggots being offered. He loosened his grip on Carole. "That thing killed our friends."

"Yes, I suppose," replied the bony figure. "Would it help you to know that it was their time?"

"What?"

The cloaked form turned around to face them. Aaron and Carole recoiled, bumping into the tree behind them. There was no flesh on the man's face, only a skull with dark eye sockets. He pulled a long scythe out of the night air and pointed it at Aaron. "When it is your time," Death said, "the circumstances are irrelevant."

Aaron pushed away from the tree. "My friends aren't irrelevant."

Death shook his head. "You don't understand." He turned away and swiftly swung himself into the saddle. "But you will."

He gripped the reins and turned his mount. From under the saddle, the bat-like wings unfolded and began to flap. Death and his mount rose off the ground, the forest floor swirling beneath them.

Aaron and Carole stood still in the center of the clearing and watched Death ascend, then disappear in an ocean of stars.

In the thin moonlight, Aaron and Carole stared at one another, unsure exactly what had just happened. After a silent moment, Carole grabbed Aaron's hand, and they started walking back to the road. They stumbled in the dark, unsure if they were heading in the right direction, twigs and debris they couldn't see snapping under their steps. Aaron searched for a tree that was smoldering, the tree Max had been sitting under, not because he wanted to gaze upon his friend's remains but because it would mean they were near the road. When he spotted it, he planned to veer away from it. Carole didn't need to see that. He didn't need to see that. But he never got the chance. They never came across a burning tree or the remains of any fire.

Like waking from a nightmare, they stepped from the woods onto the asphalt. The trees fell away, and they were again under the stars. Aaron took a deep breath, smelling pine with a hint of ash as he peered up into the night sky.

"Look," Carole said, pointing to their right.

Less than a hundred yards down the road from where they had emerged, flashing blue and red lights lit up the scene. A dozen silhouettes moved about the emergency vehicles, and before too long, one noticed Aaron and Carole standing in the road.

A flashlight was aimed their way, and then another. Aaron looked at Carole, not knowing what to feel. Her exhausted and spent features seemed to express the same emotional uncertainty. They took deep breaths, turned toward the silhouettes, and stepped toward the light.

"I'm just trying to get this straight. In your nine-one-one call, you said that only one in your party was injured," the highway patrol officer recounted. "Can you tell me why three of your friends are now deceased and appear to have expired on impact?"

Carole brought a hand to her brow. "I must have hit my head harder than I thought. I mean, I swear they were alive and talking after the crash. I guess that was just wishful thinking."

The officer flipped the page in his notebook. "Uh, huh."

Aaron could see disbelief in the officer's eyes. "Yeah, she

ran off into the woods, talking like someone was with her. I went after her, and I guess we got a little...lost." Aaron swallowed hard. Lying was not really a part of his skill set.

The officer didn't write anything down, just stared back at them.

"Hey," someone yelled from behind. "Smoking gun."

Aaron and Carole turned around, looking back at the SUV, which was no longer in the middle of the road but wrapped around an enormous pine tree. Aaron could just see Max's head slumped in the backseat, a torn airbag lying in his lap.

A fireman stood next to Collin's crushed body in the driver's seat, his girlfriend, head and all, next to him. The fireman held up an empty beer can. "There's more than one," he yelled.

"Yep, that's a shocker," said the officer taking Aaron and Carole's statement. He looked down at them, clearly not trying to hide his disdain. "You kids care to tell me how much the driver had to drink?"

Aaron met Carole's gaze. Her lips quivered, but her eyes were dead still. He couldn't tell if she was putting it together or not, but Aaron could feel the cold touch of understanding slowly washing over him.

When it is your time, the circumstances are irrelevant, Death had said.

Aaron looked the officer dead in the eyes and said, "Yeah, he had a couple of drinks." He turned his gaze to Carole. "Isn't that right, Carole?"

Carole took a breath before she answered. "Yeah," she said. "More than a couple."

The officer closed his notebook. "You two are lucky to be alive."

Aaron smiled. He knew luck had nothing to do with it. The truth was much deeper than that. He met the officer's unsympathetic eyes and said, "It wasn't our time."

A Breach in the Fence

Howling screams of anguish exploded from the back yard. Margaret bolted outside. She didn't need to see the carnage to know what was happening.

The neighbor's pit bull, a vile creature, had finally chewed its way through the decaying wood fence. It was a terror in the neighborhood and had already bitten two people—one needing stitches. Why the animal hadn't been put down was unfathomable. But past inaction wasn't paramount in her mind right now. It was the shrieks of pain painting its gory picture—and Sienna.

Margaret's only child, five-year-old Sienna, was alone in the back yard building sandcastles. Sienna was a spirited and creative child, the kind to get lost in her own world when constructing her sand structures and is not mindful enough to sense an approaching threat.

She ran to the sandbox and found it empty, save for a half-destroyed castle and a dozen dog tracks. Seeing the deep paw prints, four toes with deep gouges in the sand denoting ungroomed claws, turned her blood cold.

"Sienna!" Margaret shouted.

Her adrenaline surged as she located a blood trail. The arterial spray spattered the deck, dripped down the back steps, then continued toward the side yard. Drag marks in the dirt seemed to show a struggle. Margaret sprinted up the deck, jumped over the railing, nearly careened into the trash cans, righted herself, then dashed toward the side yard.

She found them immediately.

A blood-soaked corpse, tiny rib cage exposed, jostled as chunks of flesh were ripped from its breast. A hind leg twitched lifelessly as Sienna's head rose from behind the crimson mass, her carnivorous teeth, not yet fully formed, glazed in red gore.

"Stop it, Sienna," Margaret said, slapping her hands together. She knew she had to be stern in these moments, like her mom had been with her. "You must learn to control yourself."

Sienna's blood-soaked features turned sullen. "Sorry, mommy." She then pointed at the canine pile of exposed meat. "But he bit first."

Margaret knelt and took her only child in her arms. "I know, sweetie. One day, we'll be able to eat anything or anyone at any time. But that time is not now. Until then, we must use restraint."

Sienna gazed down at the crimson mess, one paw still twitching. "When will it be time for The Great Cutting?"

Margaret smiled. "Culling, sweetheart. The Great Culling."

Sienna looked at her mom with a cerise grin. "Culling. How much longer, Mommy?"

"Be patient, my love." She pulled Sienna close. "Soon, there won't be a fence in the world that can keep them safe from us."

The Interview

"Your son appears to be quite exceptional, Missus Warren," Dr. Ethridge said, looking up through wire-framed glasses,
his index finger pointing at the test results in front of them.
"He has the gift."

Mrs. Warren leaned forward in her seat on the other side
of the desk. "Ain't my son." She glanced to the side where seven-
year-old Anthony sat on a leather couch, entranced by his Nintendo. "My sister's kid. God rest her soul."

Ethridge watched her thin, withered fingers moving over
her chest as she made the sign of the cross. Her face was drawn,
her eyes sunken. She looked as if she hadn't slept in days.

"Perhaps your husband should join us," Ethridge said, gesturing toward the door leading to the waiting room outside his
office, where his assistant, Mrs. Anderson, sat. "I think you'll
both want to hear what this institute has to offer."

She glanced back at the door. "Naw. I think he's happier
out there. Got eyes for your secretary, he has."

Dr. Ethridge cleared his throat, trying to ignore Mrs. Warren's comment. Whatever the state of the Warrens' rural farm-

life marriage was, it certainly wasn't any concern of his. The only thing at the moment that did concern him was the boy.

"Can I have some ice cream?" Andrew said without looking up, his blond hair hanging over one eye.

"When we're done, Andy," Mrs. Warren said. She turned her tired gaze back to Ethridge, grimacing. "Can we get on with it, please?"

Ethridge pushed his glasses up. "Yes, of course." He leaned forward, glancing down at the test results. "His scores are the highest I've seen. On all levels. Telekinesis, Remote Viewing—"

Mrs. Warren snickered. "Those tests are bullshit, doctor. Findin' stars and squiggly lines on the back of cards, bending spoons. He can do that nonsense in his sleep."

There was a crash outside in the waiting room. It sounded like Mrs. Anderson had knocked her file organizer off the desk again. Second time this week.

"I'm sorry, Missus Warren. You were saying."

"I've seen him lift a tractor and hurl it into the barn like it was nothin'."

"Can I get *chocolate* ice cream?" Andrew asked.

"In a few minutes," Mrs. Warren snapped.

"A tractor?" Ethridge sat forward in his seat.

"Not just big stuff, and not just out here." She leaned forward, placing a hand on the desk. "He can move folks' insides. Blood, organs, bone."

Ethridge removed his glasses. "What?"

"Didn't that secretary of yours tell you nothing?" She lowered her voice. "It's how he lost his parents."

"Can I get hot fudge on my ice cream?" Andrew said.

"Yes, in a minute," Mrs. Warren said, glancing back at the boy, then slowly turning back to Ethridge. "The doctor that works on the dead folk, the..."

"Coroner?"

"Yes. He couldn't explain it."

"Explain what, Missus Warren?"'

"Why my sister's and her husband's hearts were turned completely 'round. Said it looked like they'd been spun like a child's toy."

Ethridge narrowed his eyes, not able to believe what he was hearing.

"We didn't think nothin' of it until Andy brought me a chicken from the barn for supper. Thought my husband had snapped its neck, but when I opened it up, it was like its gizzards had been put in a blender. They poured out like stew from a pot."

Ethridge took a deep breath and sat back in his chair. He had seen this kind of irrational fear manifested before. The guardians of these unique children were often torn between loving them and fearing them. He brought his hands up behind his head. "This is exactly the kind of thing that we enable our students to deal with. Society's misunderstanding of their gifts can cause all kinds of developmental problems."

He sat forward, peered into her exhausted eyes. "I can give Andrew a better life here. A meaningful life. One that—"

"I don't give a mule's ass 'bout what you can do for him," Mrs. Warren said through clenched teeth, lips receding, revealing discolored gums.

Ethridge was caught off guard. "If it's a matter of money—"

She slapped her hand on his desk. "We didn't come here so you could help him. We're here so you can help us."

"Help you?" Ethridge said. "Missus Warren, you have me at a slight disadvantage."

She narrowed her eyes. "Thought you were smart. Thought you'd know how to fix this. People say you folks deal with this kind of stuff. That is why we come to ya."

"Missus Warren, what is going on?"

Impatience rippled across her features. "My husband and I died two days ago, and the boy won't let us leave."

"What?"

"He's using those gifts, as you call 'em, to hold our souls inside these rotting husks, and it's painful. Painful as hell."

Ethridge chuckled. "Now, Missus Warren, please—"

"Go on," she said, laying her arm out on the desk, palm up. "You is some kind of a doctor. Find a pulse."

Better just humor her for a few minutes, he thought, until he figured out what to do. Ethridge sighed and reached for the woman's wrist. His fingers instinctively recoiled as he touched her skin.

She was cold. Real cold.

Ethridge shrugged off his initial reaction, letting his logic once again guide his actions. He reached out and took her wrist, his fingers feeling for the rhythmic sensation of flowing blood.

"You know the dead can't sleep, Doctor," she said. "I'm so goddamn tired. Never been so tired."

Ethridge wasn't getting anything. He got up, moved around the desk, and placed his hand on her neck. With his thumb, he pressed on her jugular.

Nothing.

Still refusing to believe, he leaned over and pressed the phone's intercom button. "Missus Anderson, will you go down to the ward and get me a stethoscope?" He released the button and waited for a reply.

None came.

"Missus Anderson, I need you—" He suddenly broke off as the sensation of a dog sniffing at his crotch seized his attention. He looked down and saw Mrs. Warren drawing back, her nose still sniffing the air. "Missus Warren."

"You wouldn't believe what being dead makes you hunger for, Doctor."

Ethridge stepped back, disgusted. The sooner he got the boy away from them, the better. He turned and moved toward the office door. He grasped the handle and swung it open. "Missus Anderson, I've been call..." His mouth dropped open, and his eyes bulged.

Mrs. Anderson was sprawled on her desk, dead eyes staring at the ceiling. Mr. Warren was using his hands like rib spreaders while his face sank into her exposed cavity. Ethridge could hear the sounds of chewing.

"I'll make you a deal, Doctor."

Ethridge spun around and found Mrs. Warren standing behind him, her lifeless, hungry stare boring into him.

"You get Andy to let us move on," she said, "and I won't *eat* you."

Paralyzed by horror, Ethridge watched her walk toward him. His heart pounded, and he thought it would burst from his chest. Mrs. Warren reached out for him, and he tried to raise his hands, but they remained at his side, useless.

She clutched his arms in her dead fingers and moved his stiff body out of the way. She then exited the office and joined her husband at the feast.

Ethridge staggered back, not knowing where his feet were taking him. His heels collided with the leather couch, and he plopped down into it.

The beeping sounds from Andrew's Nintendo were just a bit louder than the sounds of tearing flesh, snapping bone, and chewing resonating from the waiting room. He looked over at the boy, still peering intently into the glowing screen of the hand-held video game.

Ethridge took a deep breath. When he exhaled, he was no longer a paralyzed idiot and was once again a world-renowned parapsychologist.

"Andrew," he began.

The boy continued playing.

"Andrew, are you doing something to your aunt and uncle?"

"I don't want them to leave," Andrew said, not looking up.

"And why is that?"

"Because everyone leaves me." His forehead wrinkled. "My

dog Skipper left; mom and dad left. They left me alone."

"Tell you what," Ethridge said. "Why don't you come to live here with me and—"

"Why should I?"

He had never had to convince a child; it was always the parent or guardian who needed the persuading. "Because...because I have ice cream."

Andrew stopped playing and turned to look at him. "What flavors?"

"Oh, let me see. There is chocolate, vanilla, straw—"

"I like Rocky Road. Got that one?"

"Well, let's take a walk down to the cafeteria and see what we have. What do you say?"

Andrew stared at Ethridge, considering.

"Any progress, Doctor?" Mrs. Warren asked, stepping back into the office. Her husband was on her heels. Both corpses glared at Ethridge, hands glistening with blood, chins dripping.

Dr. Ethridge hardened his tone and tried to appear firm. "Andrew, you have to let them go. Let them go right *now*."

Ethridge could hear the dead bodies of the Warrens shuffling forward, and he tried to tune it out. He stayed focused on the boy, eyes locked. Putting a hand on Andrew's shoulder, he said, "I'm not gonna leave you. I promise." He brushed the boy's wayward strand of hair from his eyes. "You can live here and have ice cream every day."

Andrew seemed to smile. It was the first expression Ethridge had seen in the boy.

"But first," Ethridge said, seeing the Warrens' shadows fall over the couch. "You must let them go."

Andrew sighed like a kid being asked to clean his room. Then turned and faced his dead aunt and uncle. He blinked twice. "Go away."

The corpses stopped moving for an instant and just seemed to stand there like marionettes whose puppeteer had fallen asleep. Then they both slumped to the floor, their dead limbs intertwined as if in a farewell embrace. Mrs. Warren's tired eyes fluttered, then went still, her dead gaze locked on Ethridge.

Andrew jumped up, sticking the Nintendo in his pocket. Ethridge stood up slowly, eyes fixed on the bodies in his office.

"Can we go get some ice cream now?" Andrew grabbed Ethridge's hand.

The parapsychologist nodded, hoping to God that the cafeteria actually stocked some. Being a diabetic, he had never noticed. "Of course. There is a chance that they have run out. In which case we will just—"

"I hope not," Andrew interrupted. "I haven't had any since Auntie and Uncle ran out two days ago." His expression became irritated. "And that really made me mad."

Contractions

The day Aaron realized he wanted to eat his children, he knew it was time to leave. The urges were first revealed in nightmares with gruesome cinematic clarity, a horror show starring him in a reel of blood and pain. But now, the scenes of him feasting on his offspring ran in high definition in the wake of day. Like the other men before him, it was time to say goodbye before he did something no man should have to live with. No sane man could live with.

"Stay another night?" his wife said. "Just one?"

Aaron held her boneless hands and pulled her aquatic-looking limbs around him. Tears streaked her pale cheeks. "Heather, you know I can't." He brushed a wisp of hair from her face and felt the strength of her new limbs encircling him.

Like other women in town, Heather's arms had transformed. Seemingly overnight, human skin and fingers had given way to tentacles that could stretch far beyond their length. Just how far no one knew, but yesterday she had closed the front gate of the fence surrounding their property without leaving the porch.

"I would stop you," she said, "if you tried to hurt the children."

"Don't make this harder than it is," Aaron whispered. "I got the urges, and I can't stay."

Heather's arms held him like pythons, constricting, suffocating. Her cheek nuzzled the silver memento around Aaron's neck, a modest cross. She pulled back slightly. "Can't understand why you wear this. You don't even believe."

"You gave it to me," Aaron said. "That's reason enough."

She looked up into Aaron's eyes. "I don't want you to be alone when it happens. No one should be alone."

Aaron touched the cross with his fingertips. "I won't be," he said. "Iggy Patel is going with me."

Heather almost laughed. "Iggy Pat... You don't even like him."

Aaron chuckled and rested his forehead on hers. "Hate his guts." They both laughed. "Take care of our girls," he whispered. He said this knowing she would slay anyone that came near. "And if you see me again, you know what must be done."

She nodded, closed her eyes, and released her husband of fifteen years. Aaron picked up his pack and shotgun, stepped off the porch his grandfather had built, and began walking, never looking back.

As he passed through the front gate, he held an image of his family framed in his mind. His four girls, all sandy blonde, their faces peppered with cinnamon freckles, standing around their mother. He preferred to picture Heather the day he first met her, stepping off a bus from Baltimore, lost and broke; she was the most beautiful woman he'd ever seen. But her new, end-of-the-world self kept creeping in.

When Aaron first saw that her arms were transforming, he knew what it meant. It had been happening all over town; mothers went through the change just a few days before fathers began to get the insatiable hunger, the uncontrollable desire to eat children. Best Aaron could figure was that it was nature's way of trying to strike some sort of insane balance in a chaotically shifting world.

Thankful, at least, that enough was now known that he could avoid the fate of so many other families in the county—mothers clashing with fathers in an unholy custody battle. When a mother won, a father lay on the ground, often without a head. But if the father won and the kids could not get away, then everybody died. And not quickly.

It should have seemed horrific, Aaron knew, the idea of eating children. His own children. But it wasn't, and it terrified him. So much had changed in the last two months since the universe had stopped growing. No, that wasn't what they called it. Expanding, he remembered.

At first, it was believed that the global changes resulted from an industrial accident in space. But no amount of orbiting toxins could account for the fact that rocks now sometimes exploded, rabbits gathered in ferocious, carnivorous packs, and the color yellow was now painful to the touch. The last scientific expert Aaron saw on CNN, just before all broadcasts stopped, claimed the universe was now snapping back, contracting, and the laws of physics—laws that once made the world a place of reason and understanding—were now mere suggestions that nature could ignore as it saw fit.

It was as good an explanation as any other, Aaron had thought while watching the scientist illustrate his theory with an elaborate equation that he didn't have the remotest chance of understanding. But deep down, he knew nobody had a clue as to why it was all coming to such a strange end. To his mind, a physics equation couldn't explain why the trees all lived underground now or why the clouds had decided to hunt and feed on airplanes.

Iggy signaled Aaron with a gentle wave as they met up at the edge of town, neither saying more than two words to one another before heading out. Aaron stayed a good ten paces behind Iggy, hoping that the distance would discourage any notion

Iggy might be entertaining of starting a conversation. He had nothing to say to Iggy, and he hoped to God Iggy didn't have anything to say to him.

By mid-afternoon, Aaron could smell Iggy's physical efforts wafting back to him on the trail. It curled his nostrils and he lingered farther back. There wasn't much else to compete with the odor. Flowers no longer bloomed, and the fresh air didn't seem fresh anymore. Staleness rode the breeze, bringing with it the gentle reminder that it was all winding down.

Aaron was thinking about tying a bandana around his face to mask Iggy's stench when he felt the contraction coming. Just a trembling in his bowels at first, but within a few seconds, the entire planet vibrated. When a contraction came, there were two choices: hold onto something solid and try to remain standing or lie down flat on your back, eyes toward the heavens, and pray that God still gave a shit.

Letting his pack fall to the ground, Aaron dropped fast. He pressed his hands flat, palms down into the dirt, and held his breath. His guts ached; gas expanded inside him, and he felt like his head would pop. He fought against his fear to keep his eyes open. If this was it, the last and final one, Aaron wanted to see it. Face it. Gaze down its gullet and maybe catch a glimpse of what would come next.

The afternoon sky folded in on itself to the relentless pounding of thunder. Clouds appeared then vanished in the span of a moment, and just when Aaron thought it was over, the pressure came. Like weights pressing down on his body, a jolting acceleration, the entire planet became a roller coaster, plunging downward, banking hard to the right, then snapping back hard to the left.

Stomach acid burned the back of Aaron's throat. His eyeballs grew heavy; the vibrations in his skull seemed to be trying to shake away the memory of all he held dear: who he was, the girls, Heather. Then as quickly as the contraction came, it vanished with a suddenness that almost lifted him into a seated position. He exhaled fast, vomiting a little, then rolled over on his side. After wiping his mouth, he looked for Iggy. The grass and weeds were about two feet high, and if Iggy had hit the dirt, he was obscured. "Hey, Ig," Aaron called out. "You still with me?"

A quiet second passed before Aaron saw Iggy's left hand rise over the crest of the grass, delivering a very unenthusiastic thumbs-up.

"Am I crazy, or are those getting worse?" Iggy said, voice somewhat muffled by the grass.

Aaron pushed himself up and wrapped his arms around his knees. "No, I don't think that was any worse than this morning." But Aaron didn't believe that. Dealing with four young girls, he had become accustomed to downplaying almost anything put in front of him as a means of comfort. It had worked for a while, but then the contractions came.

At least that's what a physicist at some university Aaron had never heard of had decided to call them. Some other scientists had tried calling them celestial gravity subsonic inversions, but the name just didn't stick. But whatever they called them, they were getting worse. No contraction had ever produced vomit from him before, and although the pressure was always there, that last one felt like an elephant squatting on his chest.

"No, I disagree," Iggy said, beginning to stand. "I think they are getting worse." He picked up his pack. "Just wish I knew why."

Iggy was like that. Aaron remembered him from high school, always asking questions, always wanting to understand. But trying to understand the physics at the end of the world was like trying to understand why left socks always disappeared from the dryer. No one was ever gonna be able to understand why cars now drove themselves or why mountains disappeared in the night. The end of the world had its own understanding.

Iggy was near to his feet when he suddenly froze, eyes forward. Aaron tried to find what Iggy was locked onto but saw nothing. A few still beats passed as Aaron held his breath. Then Iggy craned his head back, making several quick hand gestures. They hadn't worked out any signals beforehand, but it didn't take a code breaker to surmise what Iggy was saying.

Aaron got the message. They had company.

With the ears of an experienced hunter, Aaron tuned in to the sounds. There were at least two different approach patterns: one to the right, the other dead ahead. Iggy gestured, identifying what kind of creatures were about to strike. He wiggled his fingers and forearm, mimicking the motion of a snake.

The Ones that Slither, Aaron thought. He gripped his gun, scanned the area around them, and tried not to breathe. The former mammals that had lost most of their bones usually hunted in pairs, attacking so fast victims rarely had the opportunity to scream before being swallowed alive.

Aaron motioned for Iggy to draw a bead on the one in front while he targeted the one on the right. He had just gotten his gun up and checked the sites when the tall grass moved. Flecks of auburn hair weaved in the fading sunlight, then dove like a sea serpent moving across the ocean's surface.

Aaron followed the bending grass, trying to find an opening. He soon realized that if he waited for a clear shot, it would be on him before he got a chance to fire. Narrowing his gaze, he anticipated the thing's route, took aim, and held his breath. But before he pulled the trigger, it slithered into an opening. He saw its face, mouth open, teeth bent outward, hair flapping around its scalp like alien tendrils. Glimpsing a white patch of skin on the nape of its neck, he fired.

He rocked back from the recoil, placing a hand behind him for balance. The beast's forward progress was halted, but it would not lie still. Blood sprayed like a broken sprinkler as its deformed mass thrashed in the grass.

Aaron heard Iggy's rifle fire, then the fast sound of the bolt being pulled back and slamming back again. Aaron got to his feet and saw Iggy fire once again. The thing was hit but still charged.

"Iggy, pull back," Aaron screamed, running forward and raising his gun. The thing and Iggy were so close Aaron didn't have a clear shot. "Iggy get down," Aaron ordered, heart pounding.

But Iggy held his ground, slammed the bolt forward again, and fired. The shell casing almost hit Aaron as he arrived at Iggy's side, shotgun poised to fire. Both men held still, waiting for the result of Iggy's last shot.

A hissing moan rose from the grass, then something large and furry flopped over, tail twitching, lungs gasping, then it lay still.

Aaron let out a long, hot breath as he knelt, his weight coming down much harder than he'd intended.

He looked over at Iggy, whose eyes were huge, white spheres against the backdrop of his dark olive skin. "You...," Aaron started, then decided to take a few more breaths before attempting speech again.

"You all right?"

"I think..." Iggy looked down. "I think I need to change my shorts."

"Well, damn, that sure as hell ain't gonna make you smell any better."

Iggy smiled, then laughed.

Aaron reached for Iggy's rifle. "Let me see that relic." Aaron sized up Iggy's old firearm. "Jeez, Ig, if I'd known you were gonna cover my ass with a BB gun, I'd have grabbed you my kid's slingshot."

"It's a family heirloom."

"Well, your heirloom just about ended you. Next time just hurl insults at the things."

Iggy snatched his weapon, feigning an insulted look. "Okay,

great white hunter, how'd you do?"

"I took its head nearly off," Aaron said but remembered the thing still thrashing in the grass. He put a hand on Iggy's shoulder, pushing himself up. "I'd best go check."

With his muzzle trained ahead, he returned to his firing position, then stepped over to where the blood had redecorated the grassy landscape. The thrashing had stopped, and only the breeze brought movement. Auburn hair lay still under the weight of blood and pieces of scalp liberated from the young woman's head by a shotgun blast.

Aaron pushed the head over with the barrel of the gun, allowing its dead eyes to stare skyward. Scarcely discernible as human, the eyes had been pulled around to the side of the head, like a bird or reptile. Dropping to a knee, Aaron tried to guess how young she must have been when it happened. *Fifteen, and not a day more*, he decided. The common wisdom about this phenomenon was that it happened not only across species but seemed to occur in adolescent offspring. Teenagers. The first one Aaron had killed still had the headphones from some device wrapped around its bloody and boneless neck.

"Oh, hell," Iggy said. "I think that's Gail Michener's kid."

Aaron didn't answer, and Iggy must have thought he didn't remember her.

"You know," Iggy continued, "Gail Anderson in high school."

But Aaron did remember. He'd been seeing her off and on about the same time he started dating his future wife. Not a proud moment.

"She married that drifter suddenly, remember?"

Aaron nodded, hoping that would be enough for Iggy to drop it. His chest tightened, and acid burned his throat as the history he'd denied himself flooded back. He had broken it off with Gail after falling for Heather. A few weeks later, Gail was showing early signs of motherhood beneath her waitress uniform. Then almost overnight she was married and picking out baby names. Gail never said Aaron was the father, but she had never said he wasn't. Mostly because he hadn't asked.

Aaron closed his eyes. He didn't want to see how much the auburn hair clinging to frayed pieces of scalp lying in the blood-splattered grass was the same shade as the locks on his four girls. Iggy shouldered his gun. "Didn't you go out with Gail, way back when?" Aaron took a deep breath and tried to ignore Iggy.

"Lots of people said that Michener guy wasn't the father—"

"Jesus Christ, Iggy," Aaron snapped. "You in a goddamn sewing circle?"

Iggy fell quiet and bent back a little, like grass in the breeze.

Aaron turned away. "Come on. I want a few miles between us and this mess before dark. I'll take point."

They walked in silence until Aaron's feet hurt. The sun started to set in the north this evening, and there was just enough twilight left to gather wood for a fire. They made camp at the top of a hill deep in the woods; the only sign of civilization was a fairly large farmhouse nestled a good half-mile away.

Spying it through his binoculars, Aaron could see it was occupied—at least two adults, and there was a child's swing set in the backyard. Knowing that Iggy's cannibalistic urges had started a few nights before his own, Aaron decided to keep the detail about the swing set to himself.

Both men sat down on opposite sides of the fire, pulled out the sandwiches their respective wives had prepared, and started to eat in silence. After a few bites, Aaron started to feel bad about snapping at Iggy, and since they were going to be each other's only company for the next two days, he thought he'd try to smooth things out. Lake Placid, the place where the men in the county had collectively decided to gather when the urges struck them, was a long, hard hike. And even though he didn't care much for Iggy, they needed to work together to make the journey.

"So, Ig, have you heard anything from your part of the world?"

Iggy swallowed, then frowned. "This is my part of the world. We were born in the same town, jackass."

Aaron sighed and forced himself not to reply with an insult. "You know what I mean. Anything from a relative back in India or something?"

"We haven't heard anything in a week," Iggy said. "Before Skype went down, my mom's sister said that the birds were turning back into dinosaurs." Iggy shook his head. "Most of Asia went quiet after that."

Aaron had no idea what birds had to do with dinosaurs but wasn't interested enough to ask. He took another bite and spoke from the corner of his mouth. "You believe what they say?"

"Who?"

"Scientists. The ones that say the universe is done expanding and whatnot. That these bizarre earthquakes are interstellar contractions as the universe collapses back on itself."

Iggy shook his head. "There will always be those that must find a logical and rational explanation for everything. I don't think anyone will ever know. How about you? You buy into the scientific explanation of the end of everything?"

Aaron scoffed. "Doesn't sound all that Christian to me."

"So, what do you think?" Iggy said, lowering his sandwich.

"Hell, I don't know, Ig. Maybe God's just tired. Tired of sorting it all out. Tired of keeping the Devil at bay. Tired of separating Heaven and Hell." Aaron sighed deeply. "Maybe He's just gonna let the bastard have it all."

They sat quietly for a few minutes, both men chewing slowly and staring into the fire. Images from the last few weeks ran through Aaron's mind: a jetliner that had turned to liquid over Main Street, the shrieks of a teenager as her body transformed into a slithering nightmare, and the screams of children watching their desperate parents duel. Aaron shook his head. "Sorry to bring the party down, Ig. Whatever happens, however it ends, I'm sure we will all be in Heaven soon, reunited with loved ones—

"Last night, I ate my son," Iggy said sharply, tears welling in his eyes. "Do you think there is a place for me in your Heaven?"

"Jesus, Iggy. I..."

"When my wife heard our son's screams, she stopped me before I killed him, but the boy will never walk again."

Aaron didn't know what to say. He just sat still, trying not to imagine the scene.

"Not sure why she didn't kill me. I wish she had."

Neither spoke for several minutes, both listening to the crackling fire. Finally, Aaron broke the silence.

"It wasn't your fault."

Iggy smiled, wiped at the tears that had not yet fallen. "In any case, my friend, there is no Heaven for me. Even if I am forgiven, I can never forgive myself."

Aaron was desperate to change the subject, or at least lighten the mood. Anything to chase from his mind the image of Iggy feasting on his boy's legs. He picked up some wood and fed the fire that didn't need feeding. "So what does Allah have to say 'bout all this?"

Iggy smirked and shook his head. "You're such a redneck. I'm not Muslim."

Aaron chuckled. "Okay, Buddha then."

Iggy rolled his eyes. "I'm Hindi."

Aaron shrugged. "That doesn't clear much up for me."

"No kidding." Iggy put down the remnants of his sandwich to use both hands as he continued. "My religion has many stories of the end of days via Kali and Shiva, but I think they are just stories, as this world is just a dream. Bit of a nightmare at the moment."

"The world's a dream?" Aaron said.

Iggy looked across the fire intently. "Vishnu is dreaming this world, and when he wakes, it will all be gone."

"That's a wonderful thought, Ig. You and your wife tell your kids that story before they go to bed?"

"My kids prefer Harry Potter. But I do think there is some truth to the story of Vishnu."

"Oh, do tell."

"I think what our world is experiencing is merely a changing of dreams. As one dream dies, Vishnu will give birth to another."

Aaron was quiet for a moment, wondering how seriously Iggy believed that. He looked across the fire and saw Iggy trying to hide a smirk. Then the two men both broke out laughing. Aaron chucked his stick into the fire. "Did a nifty snake-charming voodoo whistle come with that religion of yours?"

"No," Iggy said. "Glow-in-the-dark decoder ring shaped like Gandhi's head."

"Nice."

A gunshot echoed in the trees. Aaron jumped to his feet, instinctively grabbing his gun. Iggy got up a bit slower, and they stared at one another across the fire. A second, then a third shot rang out.

"Where's it coming from?" Iggy said.

But Aaron was already moving in the direction of the shots, now accompanied by distant screams. Iggy was on his heels and nearly collided with him as Aaron stopped to look down at the farmhouse.

Every light in the house was on. There was movement on the porch and billows of smoke drifting over the yard from the shotgun blasts.

Aaron took a step down the hill but felt Iggy's hand on his shoulder. "You can't go down there. You know what's happening."

Aaron took his binoculars off his hip and brought them up. He did know what was happening but still felt a perverse desire to check. Through the magnifying lens, he saw the front door fly open so hard the screen was knocked off its frame. A heavy-set woman stumbled through the opening, her appendage transformation clearly visible. One tentacle dragged on the ground behind her like a tail, tattered and torn, while the other snaked across the porch.

A blast from inside rang out, and she fell forward, down the steps, and into the yard. She flailed in the grass, trying to regain her feet.

Aaron was about to lower the binoculars when something caught his attention. Two kids, a boy maybe ten years old and a little girl not yet half that, ran into the night, toward the swing set in the backyard.

"Shit," Aaron said. "Stay here, Ig."

"Why? If you're going, I could help."

Without thinking, Aaron swung around, instinctively leveling his gun at Iggy's chest. "You know why."

Iggy took a step back and narrowed his gaze. In an instant, Aaron knew that any trust or comradery they had built had been destroyed with a simple gesture.

Iggy held up his hands. "Fine. Go."

Aaron didn't hesitate. He spun around and charged down the hill. A former high-school running back, he still had the speed of an eighteen-year-old but not the endurance. By the time he neared the farmhouse, his lungs burned, and he gasped for air.

As he entered the yard, a man limped onto the porch, using a rifle as a crutch to support a grotesquely broken leg. He shambled to the wooden steps. Aaron locked eyes with the man for a moment, but the man had no interest in him. He limped down the steps and moved toward the spot where his wife had fallen.

Something slithered in the grass, and moonlight glinted off a long tentacle as it emerged from the darkness and coiled around the man's broken leg. He screamed, then aimed at some unseen target and fired. The shot found its mark, and the woman rose from the grass, then dropped back to the ground. She twisted like dying roadkill.

Staggering, the man hobbled over to the woman, reloading

his weapon as he moved. Aaron didn't have time to call out and try to reason with the man. He got as close as he dared, steadied his aim, and fired. Hit straight through the chest, the man fell back, crimson spraying the ground.

Aaron moved forward cautiously, then stood over the man. Aaron's aim had put one near his heart, but to his amazement, the dying man started to rise. Aaron swung the butt of the gun at the man's face, connecting just below the jaw. He hadn't meant to swing that hard, but the adrenaline had consumed him. He heard the jawbone break and saw teeth fly, disappearing into the grass. The man slumped into a motionless pile of ragged clothes, blood, and broken bones.

A gurgling rose up behind him. "Gah, gah, gah."

Aaron knelt next to the woman, her only functioning tentacle flopping in the grass like a fresh catch suffocating on the deck of a fishing boat. The light was fading in her weary eyes, and Aaron gazed deep, looking for any sign of humanity. But all he saw was the raw instinct that fired a mother to protect her offspring. Animal instinct.

My God, he thought, *is this what Heather is now?* For a moment, he was glad he wasn't with her. He couldn't bear to see her become this.

"Gah, gah," she continued, tears of red outlining her cheeks.

Aaron got to his feet, preparing to use his next shot to put this animal down. He had just leveled the barrel at her forehead when a scream came from the backyard—a child's scream.

Aaron bolted around the house. He still hadn't caught his breath from his sprint but managed to reach the backyard in a few seconds. He followed the screams, now high-pitched shrieks of terror.

The children had taken refuge in a homemade fort made of plywood. But their wooden haven was under attack. Iggy had hold of the boy's leg and was pulling him free of the fort. The little girl screamed as Iggy brought his teeth down on the boy's foot.

"Iggy!" Aaron shouted, bringing the rifle up.

Stopping for a moment, Iggy met Aaron's eyes. "I can't wait. You need to try this. It's the way it's supposed to be." Like the woman in the front yard, there was nothing human in his eyes anymore. Just instinct. Just animal.

Aaron fired.

Iggy fell back into darkness, blown off his feet and into the shadows. The boy recoiled as crimson spray colored his foot.

Stepping fast, Aaron checked to make sure Iggy wasn't getting up again. He wouldn't. The shot was straight through the heart, and Aaron was relieved he wouldn't have to look him in the face and finish him. He knelt and closed the dead man's eyes.

Aaron turned and saw the boy getting to his feet. "It's all right now, son."

"Get away from me!" the boy shouted, fear visibly rippling in his body.

"I ain't gonna hurt you, boy," Aaron said.

"Daddy," the little girl said as she bolted out of the fort and into Aaron's arms.

Aaron let his gun fall so he could embrace the girl.

"Carrie, that's not Dad," the boy shouted. "Get away from him."

Aaron could feel the child trembling, and he rubbed her back softly. "Is your name Carrie?"

She looked up at him with tear-streaked eyes and nodded.

"Well, I have a little girl named Carrie." Aaron smiled. "She is a little older, but..." Aaron inhaled deeply. "She smells just like you."

The images of his girls flooded his mind, the way they talked, the way they moved. The sound of their laughter echoed in his memory. "Just like you," he said.

He brushed her hair with his hand, which seemed to calm her the way it did a chicken right before its head was lopped off.

"There, there. No more tears." Aaron was surprised at how soothing his voice had become. And then he had an outlandish thought. An alien idea at first, but it also made a strange kind of sense. He wondered how much pressure it took to bite through a child's skull. Could he do it in one try, or would he have to gnaw on it like a dog chewing a bone? If he could get the angle right—

"Get away from her," came a voice far outside his thoughts. He felt something strike the side of his head, and as he fell back, he saw the boy's silhouette swinging his gun.

With his back flat on the ground, Aaron felt it first. The earth was beginning to shake. Another contraction was coming. Looking up at the stars, now tracers of dotted light, he shouted, "Kids, get down!"

He couldn't see if they obeyed as the bone-breaking pressure came much faster this time, heavy and violent. He tried to turn his head, but the blow to his skull sent pain down his neck. With his gaze locked straight up, he had a spectacular panoramic view of a once-in-a-trillion millennium event blossoming directly overhead.

The blurry lines of stars winked out like dying lightbulbs in a distant and unreadable marquee. Then, thin at first, a glowing line bisected the night sky, dilating as it stretched across and beyond Aaron's vision.

The Milky Way-sized fissure began to open, ripping the heavens in half.

Aaron peered into the chasm, unable to move, unable to blink, and saw all the way back to the beginning of everything, gestating in a passageway that was impossible to know. But deep down, in every cell, every atom that comprised his insignificance, he did know it. Aaron had stood by and watched hundreds of domesticated animals come into this world, held his wife's hand as she delivered their four girls. Aaron knew a birth canal when he saw one.

The Earth pressing at his back became less violent, as if the part of the planet he was on had detached from the rest. The air was thin. He gasped for each breath, and his lungs began to ache. Still unable to blink and not wanting to, he watched as the remaining stars fell into the enormous opening above, like marbles rolling off an uneven table.

Summoning up the last vestige of control he had over his body, he brought a hand up to his chest, dug under his shirt, and grasped the cross Heather had given him. It didn't offer comfort or understanding, just the memory of her and his girls. He clutched it so tight the silver edges cut into his skin. Then from above, something began to emerge.

Forcing its way through, it pushed, tore at the boundaries of the canal, destroyed the passage as it came into being. It was fire and ice, the beginning and the end, everything and nothing, and it exploded into existence with a shriek of pain and cosmic awareness. It was the end of one dream and the beginning of another.

Aaron laughed. Not because he found anything funny, but because he gleaned understanding. Not much, but it was enough. "Congratulations," Aaron whispered, squeezing the cross with all he had left. "It's a Universe."

Green Eyes and
Chili Dogs

Dale stared down at death. It wasn't the first time, and until his arteries finally petrified from a lifetime of truck-stop cuisine, it wouldn't be the last.

No more than twenty, the girl lay on an autopsy table. Not the modern stainless steel variety, but a porcelain antique with aluminum legs and a drain similar to the kind found in the average bathtub.

Dale hovered over the grisly scene. For a few seconds, he thought he might be dead, too, just a disembodied apparition. Then the chili dogs he had wolfed down a few hours ago started doing unpleasant things to his insides. Even though he gazed down at a young woman frozen in death during what he assumed was a premature autopsy, it was the chili dogs causing waves of nausea to ripple through him. Swallowing back the discomfort, he reached out for the poor girl.

Despite a thick layer of makeup, her face had an innocent, endearing quality. He wanted very much to close those green eyes, give this one some peace, and let the ferryman know she was ready for the final journey. But his hand disappeared into her cheek, emerging out the other side.

That's when Dale knew it was merely a dream. It made sense. Most everything was grainy, out of focus, black and white, except for those piercing green eyes. He took a deep breath and willed himself to consciousness. *Damn it, Dale. Wake the hell up.*

He opened his eyes, then shut them again, stunned by the glare of oncoming headlights. Bringing a hand over his brow, he opened his eyes slowly, like a child cautiously opening a closet door, unsure of what's inside.

"Hey, hey, welcome back sunshine," a husky voice to his left said.

Glancing over, Dale saw Earl in the driver's seat of the eighteen-wheeler. His friend and sometimes partner, unshaven, grinned at him with tobacco-stained teeth. Earl's gut would have done Santa Claus proud. It pressed up against the steering wheel, and his stretched-to-the-limit t-shirt could barely contain it.

"You get enough beauty sleep, partner?" Earl said.

Dale yawned.

Answering his own question, Earl said, "Nope, didn't think so. Still look like three-day-old road kill."

Dale heard a feminine laugh behind him. He turned around and looked behind his seat. A young woman bent forward, hand over her face, giggling.

"Oh, Dale, this here is Katy. Picked her up about twenty miles back."

Katy offered her hand. "Hi. I really appreciate the lift. Was out there for hours. Thought I'd have to sleep next to a cactus."

"Uh, yeah. No problem," Dale said, taking her soft hand, and gazing into her green eyes. Without letting go, he turned to Earl. "Pull over."

Earl frowned. "What's wrong?"

Dale let go of her hand. "Just pull over."

"Damn, if you need to drain the lizard, put your knees together for a mile or two," Earl said. "There's a chew and choke just up the—"

"Now, Earl," Dale said. "I gotta go now."

"Fine." Earl started to downshift. "I swear you got the bladder of a ninety-year-old woman. Hell, we oughta invest in some of them adult diapers so we could get a haul in on time."

The tires rolled over the gravel along the side of the highway, and before the rig had stopped, Dale opened his door. He jumped out of the cab, his boots touching down in the Utah desert.

At half past midnight, it was pitch-black outside, but the lights from the rig did a fair job of chasing away the darkness in a ten-yard perimeter. Dale walked straight for the point where light faded into night, kicking up dust under his heavy footfall. He wasn't a fat man, but no one had ever accused him of missing a meal. Dale unzipped his fly and pissed into the breeze.

"What the hell is so damn urgent?" Earl took position next to Dale. "I swear, sometimes you're jumpier than bull's testicles on snippin' day."

"Why'd you pick her up?"

"You're not gonna give me the 'Never pick up hitchhikers speech,' are ya? She can't be more than a hundred and ten pounds. Hell, I think we can take her."

"No, it's not that."

"What then?"

"I... I just saw her."

Earl shook his head. "You couldn't have. You've been sawing logs since Barstow, buddy."

Dale looked down, tapped, and sighed. "No. I saw her in a dream."

A grin curled up Earl's cheeks. "Yeah, I dream about young things like that all the time. Once there was this—"

"Not that kind of dream, you cradle-robbing shithead," Dale snapped. "I mean she was...stripped naked. Cut up like a high school dissection project."

Earl lowered his voice, glancing back at the cab. "You saw her naked?"

"Old man, will you please focus?"

"Sorry." Earl zipped up.

"I think she's in danger or...something." Dale sighed. "Just a feeling."

Earl didn't respond for a few moments, distant crickets filling the silence. "Oh Lord, how I hate it when you get a feeling," Earl said. "Well, if she stays with us, we can look after her."

"Yeah, I suppose. I hate this kind of crap."

Earl leaned close to Dale. "Did you get a chance to check out the headlights on her?"

Dale could picture them, but not at all like Earl probably was. In Dale's vision, her round breasts were no longer held in place by firm, uncut skin. They had flopped to either side of her chest and rested on blood-soaked porcelain.

"Jeez, Earl. You're old enough to be that girl's estranged, drunken, perverted, unshaven, don't-even-invite-him-over-for-Thanksgiving-no-more grandfather."

Earl raised his voice. "Unshaven?" He turned his head so Dale could see his face in profile. "This is trimmed and deliberate stubble." Earl ran a hand over his cheeks and double chin. "I think it makes me look like that Ethan Hawke. What do you think?"

Dale felt vile rumblings deep in his belly and splashes of vomit burning his throat. "Hell, I don't know, Earl. When Ethan is in his late fifties and puts on seventy pounds, I'll let you know."

If he got moving, he might be able to quell the need to puke, so Dale started walking back to the truck.

"Jeez, Dale. Can't ya ever say anything nice to me?"

Dale stopped. *Damn, he's needy.* Without turning around, he said, "You don't smell god-awful today. How's that?"

"Now, was that so hard? Swear to God, good buddy, getting a compliment out of you is more difficult than circumcising a honey badger."

Before Dale could take another step, he felt a massive belch ascend his esophagus. He tried to swallow it, but it burned like raw jalapenos. He instinctively bent forward, just in time to avoid puking on his boots.

Earl placed a hand on his heaving back. "Ya see, that's why you're not supposed to eat more than one of them chili dogs at that place. Hell, even the waitress said so."

Katy yelled from the cab. "Is he all right?"

"Oh yeah," Earl said. "If puking yer guts out ever becomes an Olympic event, my friend here will win that gold medal faster than you can say. 'Ohhhweee, what's that smell?'"

Feeling a great deal better and ten pounds lighter, Dale wiped his mouth. "Well, that was fun."

"If you're all done redecorating Utah, I suggest we get this show back on the road."

Dale held out his hand. "I'll drive."

Earl pulled out the keys. "All right, but be gentle with her this time. My rig's a Peterbilt lady, unlike that Mack whore you tool around in."

Earl was baiting him into another smack-talking session over whose truck was superior, but he wasn't in the mood. His throat burned like hell, every breath he took reeked of chili, and there was a girl in the cab he could easily picture with her chest cracked open. He just wanted this run to be over.

Dale sparked the engine back to life while Earl let out a long belch. The unwelcome odor of chili filled the cab. Earl rubbed his belly and made a sour face.

"How many of those chili dogs did you have?"

"Just one," Earl said.

"Well," Dale said, pulling back out onto Interstate 15. "It's probably gonna take a little longer."

"No, sir," Earl shook his head. "I ain't puking. Only girls puke. No offense ta either of ya."

Katy chuckled behind them.

"So where are ya headed, Katy?" Dale asked.

"Back home," she said. "Salt Lake City."

Christ, Dale thought. Few places on the planet gave Dale the willies, but Salt Lake City always made his hair stand on end. Even in broad daylight, the city just seemed off kilter. All the streets spun out from the cathedral, like the spires in a web, trying to snare a meal for some unseen spidery god.

"So do you guys drive together all the time?" Katy asked. "I mean, I've seen truckers ride together before, but it's usually a man and wife team. Oh, unless you guys are..."

Detecting apprehension in her voice, Dale said, "Are what?"

"Well, I don't judge or anything." Her voice quivered. "And not that there's anything wrong with that."

Dale finally got her meaning. It must have hit Earl at the same time because they both responded with a deep and masculine, "No!"

"God, no," Dale continued.

In the rearview mirror, Dale saw Katy wave her hands as she said, "Like I said, not judging."

Earl laughed, then belched.

Dale fanned the smell of regurgitated chili with his hand. "Will you stick a cork in it? Jeez."

Earl rubbed his belly. "Better out, than in." He turned around. "See, Katy, we're just doing a double-haul. Did ya notice we got two trailers hooked together?"

"Uh, yeah," Katy said.

"The one on the end is his." Earl gestured to Dale. "Sometimes cargo needs to get from L.A. to Chicago in an awful hurry. With just one driver, that can take near three days iffen the driver is obeying the law. With two drivers, Dale and I can go straight on through, cutting the time in half."

"Get there faster," Katy said.

"And pays triple." Earl grinned.

The headlights lit up a sign, which Dale squinted to read. Salt Lake City 12 miles.

Earl leaned toward Dale. "She thought that you and me—"

"I got it, Earl," Dale snapped.

Earl sat back up straight. "Iffen I swung that way, I could get someone prettier than you." He turned to face Katy. "Don't you think I could get someone prettier than him?"

Katy laughed. "I don't know. Maybe."

"What do you think of this stubble?" Earl said. "Think I look a bit like that Ethan Hawke?"

"Yeah, a bit," Katy said.

Earl turned toward Dale. "Told ya."

Good God. Dale contemplated driving into a set of oncoming headlights. "So Katy," he said, catching her gaze in the rearview mirror. "What brings ya home?"

"Oh..." She slumped back into her seat. "My mom called me. Wants me to help with Billy, my younger brother."

"He sick?" Dale asked.

"No, just acting funny."

Earl turned around. "Funny, how?"

"Ever since he graduated from high school, couple months back, he just sleeps all day."

"Oh hell," Earl said. "That's just being lazy. Post-graduation syndrome."

"It's not just that," Katy continued. "Mom said he never eats anymore. He's turned pale and thin. And when he does go out, it's only after dark."

A chill crawled up Dale's spine. He glanced over at Earl, who was looking back at him. Dale could tell they were thinking the same thing.

"Mom says his whole personality has changed—like he's a different person. And he has this new group of friends Mom has never seen before." Katy paused.

Dale met her gaze in the mirror. The luster of her green eyes faded.

Katy shrugged. "I don't know. Mom thinks that I can talk some sense into him. We used to be close."

Mentally, Dale kicked himself. There was a silver cross in the glove box of his truck, kept for just such an emergency. But they weren't in his truck. They were in Earl's. Dale had no idea what implements Earl kept on hand, beyond a Bowie knife— one as big as a machete.

Katy rested her elbows on the back of their seats. "Hey, listen. You guys have been real nice to me, and I'm sure my mom wouldn't mind if you wanted to come in for a minute. Use the facilities, grab a bite to eat."

Earl let go with another belch, patting his stomach. "Nothing to eat, thank you, but I could use a quick shower."

"Sure," Katy said, turning toward Dale. "How about you?"

Dale sighed, wishing he were still asleep.

"Well, how about it?" Earl said.

"Sure, why not," Dale said, putting on the turn signal. He eased the rig over, taking the first exit into Salt Lake City.

A few minutes later they parked on a faintly lit suburban street. The houses were big—two and three stories—and even in the night, Dale could see finely manicured landscaping.

Katy hopped down. "Just let me go in first and say hi. Then I'll wave you in, okay?"

"Yeah, sure." Earl closed the cab door. Turning to Dale, he lowered his voice. "Think we should let her go in alone?"

"I think her story has already been written, my friend."

"Huh?"

Dale shook his head. "Never mind."

They both watched in silence as Katy crossed the street and followed the walk to a two-story Victorian. The dark porch seemed to swallow her petite form. She had been out of sight for a full minute before either of them spoke.

"How long we gonna sit here?" Earl rubbed a hand over his stubble.

Dale looked up the street. The ghost-white steeples of the Mormon temple rose like watchtowers, keeping a vigil on its flock. The looming spires added to Dale's discomfort, reminding him that there were a million places he'd rather be about now. "Guess that's long enough." He turned to Earl. "Whatcha got?"

Earl reached under the seat and pulled out a heavy vinyl carrying case rolled up like a sleeping bag. As Earl unfurled it, Dale was pleasantly surprised to see that Earl was better prepared than he'd imagined. Throwing-knives, a handgun, bullets— some silver, some not—and several sets of brass knuckles were all tucked in to form-fitting pouches.

"I'll take the thirty-eight," Dale said, removing the revolver. He flipped open the carousel, checking to see if it was loaded. It was.

As he tucked the gun in the small of his back behind his belt, Earl pulled out two throwing knives and shoved them in his back pocket. He reached under the seat again and came up with a Bowie knife cradled in both hands.

Dale smiled as he read the large inscription on the blade. BETSY.

"You ready to go to work, old girl?" Earl said to his knife.

Dale slapped Earl's arm. "Come on, old man."

As they crossed the street, Earl let go another chili-laced burp. Dale frowned at him. "More stealth, less belching."

Earl feigned a salute, and they moved up the walk. The wooden porch creaked under their considerable weight. In the stillness of the night, it seemed thunderous. Dale put his hand on the door. It was ajar. He took a deep breath and pushed.

The door swung inward, and they both stared for a moment. There were only two sources of light in the house. One came from upstairs, very faint, distant—probably escaping from underneath a closed door. The other was bright and glaring.

Dale got the impression that it was a light bulb hanging free with no lampshade to soften the glow. It shone upward, and although Dale couldn't see the source, it was coming from a cellar.

Gesturing with Betsy, Earl said, "Age before beauty."

Dale moved inside. His boots made no sound as he stepped onto a thick throw rug. Following his instincts, he headed toward the cellar, motioning Earl to follow.

The cellar light, at the end of a wide hall, illuminated family photos on the wall. Dale recognized images of Katy, with someone he assumed was her younger brother. The siblings were pictured at different moments in their lives—elementary school, soccer team pictures, proms. As he moved down the hall, taking in the images was like watching them grow up.

When Dale reached the cellar entrance, he glanced back at Earl before he started his descent. He had no doubt that Earl would always be there, covering his back, ready to take on whatever horror awaited them, but he still felt the need to check. They both took a deep breath and then descended.

Midway, Dale hunched to get a better view and caught sight of four aluminum table legs sitting dead center on the cement floor. With one more step, he saw the white porcelain of the autopsy table. He paused for a moment and closed his eyes.

"You okay?" Earl put a hand on Dale's shoulder.

Dale nodded, swallowed hard, and opened his eyes.

Stepping onto the cellar floor, each moved to opposite sides of the porcelain table. They stared down at Katy and her green eyes.

"Oh, sweet Jesus." Earl wiped his brow.

Dale knew this is what they would find, but a small part of him, now crumbling into disappointment, wanted to be surprised. She looked cold, and he wanted to cover her somehow. But her days of feeling cold were long gone.

"I don't get it," Earl said. "This couldn't have happened in five goddamn minutes. This took hours to do."

Dale nodded. "I know."

"And if she's been lying here—" Earl paused, swallowing. "Who the hell did we have in my rig?"

Dale just shrugged.

Earl shuddered as if a ghost had just moved through him. "How in the hell does this creepy shit always find us? I mean, it's not like we go looking for it."

Dale examined the two small puncture wounds in Katy's neck, very round and deep. "We're just lucky that way, I guess."

"So, what now?" Earl said. "Get outta here? Make an anonymous call to Johnny Law?"

Dale shook his head. "Katy didn't bring us here just to find her."

"Afraid you were gonna say that." Earl sighed. "So what's the plan?"

"Check the rest of the house. If we don't find nothin', then we wait."

"Great," Earl said. "I always wanted ta—"

They both jumped as an old rotary phone mounted on the wall began to ring.

Dale pointed the .38 at the phone; his finger wrapped tight around the trigger guard. Upstairs, at least four other phones were ringing in unison, some with electronic bleeps, others with a traditional ring.

After the fourth ring, Earl said, "Are ya gonna shoot the phone?"

Dale rolled his eyes and lowered the pistol.

"You want I should get that? It might be our bad guy calling to say hey." Earl grinned.

Before Dale could respond, the ringing stopped. It didn't stop because the caller had given up, terminating the connection. It stopped ringing because someone answered it.

Dale and Earl exchanged silent, wide-eyed glances.

Someone upstairs, possibly on the second floor, had picked up, and Dale could make out a male voice, filtering down through the still house.

"No. I was just getting a little rest," the voice said. "I can't wait to be with you again, my beloved."

Dale heard feet slap down above as if someone was getting out of bed—or a coffin.

"Yes, it did take a long time," the voice continued. "Mother, too. But it was well worth it. They tasted divine—like black roses harvested from graveyard soil."

Heavy steps moved above. The voice got louder as the footfalls began to descend the stairs.

"You did?" The voice sounded excited. "How delicious."

Dale motioned for Earl to take position under the stairs on the right. Dale stood to the left.

The voice was now at the top of the cellar stairs, and the words were crystal clear. "Until we are together again, my dark princess. For I am but only half a demon without you."

Dale had the nauseating feeling of listening to a horror romance novel on tape, complete with cheesy goth dialogue. Worst of all, he was almost sure what the creep would say next, and he cringed at the thought. *Don't say it, please don't say it.*

"You complete me," the voice said at the top of the cellar stairs.

God, I can't wait to kill this son-bitch.

Dale heard the soft beep of a cordless phone being switched off, and then heavy footsteps shook the wooden stairs as the man descended. Dale pressed himself against the wall, sucking in his gut. Earl did the same, with little effect.

A dark figure stepped down onto the cellar floor, a black silk cape trailing behind him. Shoulder-length hair the color of midnight swayed with the creature's movements as it approached Katy's body. He reached out a bony hand and caressed her dead cheek.

"We still have so much more to do, my sister." The monster was Katy's younger brother, Billy. He moved to the other side of the table, his ebony eyes aimed at Katy's dead green ones. "We've only just begun this journey, you and I. Together we will explore passions only dreamt about in the—"

Earl interrupted the bastard's monologue with a loud, unrestrained belch.

He looked over at Dale and said, "Sorry."

The dark figure stood erect, about five and a quarter feet tall. Dale registered a hint of surprise on the creature's face. Billy wore a dark pinstriped vest with a tuxedo-style collar. Blood-red jewels dangled from a choker around a milky-white neck streaked with veins.

Billy raised his arms dramatically, flinging the cape off his shoulders. He bared one-inch fangs that gleamed ivory under the naked light bulb.

Jeez, Dale thought. *Somebody's got Dracula envy.*

"Foolish mortals," Billy said. "Rushing down into a dark lair, knowing not what you'll find."

"Yeah," Dale said. "We're kind of stupid that way."

Billy, now a blood-lusting thing, stepped away from the table. "Do you know whose presence you're in?"

"Enlighten us." Earl brought up the knife.

Billy narrowed his gaze, and his black pupils were just visible between slits of pale skin. He tilted his head down, revealing a Bela Lugosi hairline. "I am a God of Death."

Dale chuckled.

"You mock me, sir?"

"Sorry," Dale said. "I just thought that iffen I ever met a god, he'd be... ya know." Dale looked at Earl. "Help me out, buddy."

"Taller?" Earl said, raising an eyebrow.

"Yeah." Dale agreed, taking aim with the .38. "Taller."

Billy hoisted his arms like a Shakespearean thespian demanding the audience's attention. "Like the night, I am forever. Long after this earth has reclaimed your bodies, I will continue in the darkness, forever employed by death, draining the living for my unending journey through time. I am eternal. I am the night. I am forever—"

Dale shot Mr. Forever through the forehead.

Billy fell back against the rear wall and slid downward. Like a slug, he left a thick, pulpy trail. Astonishment chiseled on his dead features.

Earl moved fast for a man his size, approaching Billy's body. He knelt and looked as if he were going to poke the boy with Betsy.

"Easy, Earl." Dale kept the pistol trained on Billy's unmoving chest. "That ain't always the end of them."

"Careful is my middle name." Earl brushed the blade across Billy's cheek.

Dale lowered the gun. "Your middle name is Marion."

"Now, I told you that in confid— What the hell?" Earl rotated the blade, revealing a dull white substance on its edge.

A flesh-colored spot had appeared were Earl had scraped the knife. Earl rubbed his thumb across Billy's neck, smearing the stenciled-on veins. His thumb glistened with makeup.

"You gotta be kidding me." Earl opened the dead boy's mouth. He yanked out one of the fangs. Holding up the dislodged prosthetic tooth, he shook his head. "You crazy sonbitch." He turned to Dale. "What the hell is wrong with kids today?"

Dale sighed, putting the pistol back in his belt.

Earl stood and tossed the porcelain fang onto Billy's chest. "I mean, why can't they just raid their parent's liquor cabinet and smoke pot like we did?"

Dale moved forward, looking down at Katy's green eyes. They were the prettiest shade of forest he had ever seen.

"I swear, Dale, video games, social media, reality TV—it's rotting their little brains." Earl's voice rose. "Get up, you son-bitch. It's my turn ta kill ya."

"You about through?"

Earl rubbed his forehead. "Yeah." He joined Dale at the table. "Sure was a sweet thing."

Dale said, "An angel if ever there was one." He closed her eyes with his fingers. "Sleep now, child."

Earl crossed his hands over his belly, and both men stood silently with only the sound of their breathing between them.

The sound of the front door closing echoed upstairs. Dale froze. Footsteps moved over the ceiling, heading for the cellar stairs.

Dale and Earl turned to face the door. Within moments, a set of long female legs encased in thigh-high patent leather boots came into view. They seemed a bit unsteady, as if the owner was carrying something, making the journey down the steps awkward. When the woman reached the bottom level, she froze, surprise showing through a pound of goth-styled makeup.

She held a bundle two feet long, limp and unmoving. It was a child. The bright pink *Dora the Explorer* pajamas contrasted sharply with the woman's Vampira outfit.

"I'll be dammed," Earl said. "There's a Missus Son-bitch."

Without a word, the woman dropped the child. Dale lurched forward, arms outstretched. He missed the child's body but caught her head, keeping it from hitting the cement floor. The woman scrambled up the stairs.

Dale pulled the girl to his chest as he felt something pass over his head, nicking his hair. One of Earl's throwing knives stuck in the thick black heel of Vampira's boot.

The blade didn't slow her down.

Earl grimaced apologetically.

"Get that child-stealin' bitch," Dale yelled.

Earl rushed past Dale and mounted the stairs. "Look out,

wide load coming through."

Dale held the child out in front of him. "Please don't be dead." He placed a thick finger on the small neck, holding his breath.

The child was breathing, and he felt a strong pulse in her neck. He gasped with relief. "Thank you."

He leaned in and caught the familiar scent of chloroform. "Goddamn sons-a-bitches."

The child stirred. He brushed her beautiful auburn locks away from her eyes and stood up. "You just get some rest, sweetie. Ain't nothing gonna hurtcha now."

Dale looked back at Katy, now understanding why she had brought them here. "You done real good, girl. Real good." Then he headed up the steps.

In the living room, Dale found a loveseat close to the entryway. He gently deposited the sleeping child and pulled an afghan over her. "I need to go help Uncle Earl, but I'll be back," he whispered.

Dale hurried through the open front door. He took out the pistol, looking up and down the street for any sign of Earl or Vampira. On the last porch step, he felt something slick under his boot. Both feet went out from under him. He braced for impact. Ass first, he hit the brick walkway.

"Goddammit." Dale rolled off one cheek, the stench of chili assaulting his nostrils.

"Oh hell, Dale, I'm sorry." Earl strolled across the lawn.

"What'd I slip on?"

Earl stood over him, rubbing his belly. "I come up them basement steps so darn fast it jarred something loose. That chili dog just did a Mount Saint Helens on me."

Dale realized what he was sitting in. "Aww, man..." He sat back down. "Well, did ya get her?"

Earl shook his head. "Sorry, buddy. Twenty years ago, maybe." He slapped his gut. "This body was built by Bud."

"Dammit, Earl."

"Hey, I ain't no Mark Spitz or nothing."

Dale furrowed his brow. "What?"

"Ya know, that Olympic running guy."

"Mark Spitz was a swimmer, you idiot."

"Oh." Earl scratched his head. "Who am I thinking of? Olympics, fast running fella."

"I have no idea." Dale thrust his hand up at Earl.

Earl grasped Dale's hand and pulled him up. There was a wet sound as Dale's butt departed the walk.

Dale stood, slapping regurgitated chili off his ass. "Exactly why am I friends with you?"

"Because I'm so damn pretty." Earl grinned. But looking back at the house, his expression turned solemn. "Is the little one, I mean is she—"

"No," Dale said. "Just sleeping. Chloroform."

Earl let out a long breath. "What now? Can't call the local cops. We'd be here for the next few days trying to reckon all this."

"Yeah, and I'm not looking forward to explaining how we come to be here, neither."

"What then?"

Dale thought for a moment. "I still know a few folks at the FBI. One I know would keep my report of what went on here anonymous. At least the info would get filtered down to the locals."

"What about the little one? Can't leave her here."

Dale gazed out across the yard, seeing the enormous white spires in the distance. "I got an idea."

"The FBI, huh." Earl slapped his belly. "I know you don't like to talk about it, but one day you're gonna have to tell me more about this life you had before we met."

Dale slapped Earl's back. "Now, you know my life didn't really begin 'til I met you." He moved up the steps.

"As much as I appreciate the sweet talk," Earl said, "I know you're just trying ta change the subject. Again."

After depositing the sleeping child on the top step of the temple, Dale looked back only once. When security guards swarmed around the bundle, he said a silent goodbye.

Dale made his way to where Earl waited in the truck, engine humming. He hopped into the cab.

"Everything go all right?" Earl said.

"Just fine."

Earl turned the lights on as the truck began to roll forward. "If I might make a personal observation, good buddy?"

Dale buckled up, sighing. "If you must."

"For a man as religiously void as you is, that was a very spiritually insightful thing you just done."

Dale folded his arms and sank into his seat. "Will you please just get me out of Utah?"

"That suits me, and there's this all-night diner on the other side of the state line, fries up the best—"

"You just puked," Dale said, looking at Earl in amazement.

Earl patted his belly. "I know. Now I got all this room. Ya see..."

Dale shook his head, tuning out Earl's annoying drone. He wanted so badly to go to sleep. He wanted so badly for this run to be over. Shutting his eyes, he attempted to will himself unconscious. It didn't work.

He gazed out his window and imagined that he saw green eyes dimly reflected in the glass.

Good Night, Katy.

For more Earl and Dale, check out *Midnight Men: The Supernatural Adventures of Earl & Dale.*

ABOUT THE AUTHOR

Kevin David Anderson currently lives in Southern California. Before becoming a writer, Anderson earned a B. A. in Mass Communication (TCOM) with a focus on Media Production from CSUF (Fresno State). He worked as a marketing professional for more than a decade, during which he managed award-winning campaigns for both television and radio.

Anderson's debut novel, the geeky, cult zombie classic *Night of the Living Trekkies* is a funny, offbeat zombie novel exploring the pop culture carnage that ensues when the undead crash a Star Trek convention. The Washington Post listed it as one of the top five Zombie novels of 2010.

Night of the Living Trekkies and Anderson's follow up, *Night of the ZomBEEs*, have become required reading in college courses, most notably the class designed for incoming freshman, *How to Survive Your Freshman Year by Studying the Zombie Apocalypse*, at Mansfield University in Pennsylvania.

Anderson's short stories have appeared in almost a hundred publications, from anthologies and magazines to podcasts and radio dramas, in multiple languages and on every continent, excluding Antarctica. Anderson was the first American to be published in the award-winning South African Horror Magazine, *Something Wicked*. Dozens of his stories have been turned into audio productions by voice talents like Jason Hill, Rish Outfield, and Mur Lafferty, on Parsec Award-winning podcasts like Pseudopod, The Drabblecast, The Dunesteef, and on the very popular Simply Scary Podcast and the No Sleep Podcast.

Anderson also produces pop culture joke books for fans of all ages under the pen name Giggles A. Lott & Nee Slapper. Titles include *The Geektastic Joke Book 4 Kids, Jurassic Jokes: A Book 65 Million Years in the Making, Star Wars: The Jokes Awaken,* and the Star Trek-themed *Deep Space Jokes: Going where no joke book has gone before...*

For more information on Anderson visit KevinDavidAnderson.com.

Reprint Acknowledgments

Midnight.

The Witching Hour.

But the creatures of darkness are not
confined to the shadows of the night.
Lonely stretches of highways…
Bustling college campuses…
Quiet suburban neighborhoods…
Pricey, upscale day spas…
They're everywhere.

Earl and Dale, a pair of burly truckers,
seem to be drawn to those that dwell in the darkness.
Monster hunters by default, they
confront the evil fearlessly—and with just a bit of humor.
Vampires, werewolves, half-human spider demons,
and those that prey on the innocent…
All will realize they've met their match
when they go head to head with…

The Midnight Men

CPSIA information can be obtained
at www.ICGtesting.com
Printed in the USA
BVHW092355181122
652278BV00021B/1971